THIS FREEDOM JOURNEY

THE MOUNTAIN SERIES ~ BOOK 8

MISTY M. BELLER

Misty M. Beller

BOOKS

The characters and events in this fictional work are the product of the author's imagination. Any resemblance to actual people, living or dead, is coincidental.

Unless otherwise indicated, all Scripture quotations are taken from the Holy Bible, Kings James Version.

ISBN-13 Trade Paperback: 978-0-9997012-5-6

ISBN-13 Large Print Paperback: 978-1-954810-39-6

ISBN-13 Casebound Hardback: 978-1-954810-40-2

I will lift up mine eyes unto the hills, from whence cometh my help?
My help cometh from the Lord, which made heaven and earth.

Psalm 121:1-2 (KJV)

CHAPTER 1

This journey I take seems foolish to others, yet I can't help the yearning that fuels me.
~ Adrien's Journal

*A*drien Lockman trudged through the snow, the frames of his snowshoes carrying him at least two feet higher than the weary mule tracking behind him. Mountains rose on either side, but this narrow gap between the rock cliffs kept the wind from badgering them. Much.

Maybe he should try to build a shelter between these mountains to spend the rest of the winter. Protection on two sides was better than nothing. And he'd have access to the hot springs he'd stumbled on the day before. Water any time he needed, even though the stuff smelled murky.

But something drove him onward. Maybe the fact that these

winter months were the last chance he would allow himself to explore unfettered. When spring came, he'd be building a house in that wide valley he'd found a couple days before. That open land spread far enough to raise a host of cattle and horses. Live life on his own terms. He'd have responsibilities, but the kind of his own choosing.

Until then, he planned to cover as much ground as he could. Explore as far into these great rocky peaks as his snowshoes would take him.

Wind gusted against his face, blowing up a cloud of icy pellets covering the ground. At least only a little snow was falling from the sky today.

He pulled his fur cape higher over his face so only a slit for his eyes was open to the elements. As he pushed on, the wind battered more, blowing its cold fury to sting his eyelids.

The blinding white swirled around him, thick enough so the cliffs beside him vanished. How much fell from above and how much was blown up from below became impossible to decipher. The brutal icy air churned like a dense cloud restricting his ability to judge distance.

Should he stop and wait for the wind to die down? The biting cold had benumbed his limbs, giving him little choice. He wouldn't last much longer in these fierce elements without shelter.

He continued forward and to the right, reaching out to feel the cliff side before he ran into it. Poor Domino trudged behind him, soldiering on. The reluctant mule must have resigned himself to freezing to death some time yesterday, when he'd stopped balking at the belly-high snow.

After a dozen strides, Adrien's hand still hadn't struck the wall of mountain that spanned them on the right. Perhaps the cliff had tapered to a low hill at this point. The snow swirled thick—so thick he could only make out objects a few feet ahead.

He stopped, then turned to his left toward the cliff that held court on that side of the narrow trail. He progressed a dozen strides that way. Where was the mountain?

The first solid stab of fear twisted in his chest.

Oh, God. Have mercy on me.

He had to find one of those cliff walls. Or maybe the cliffs were gone now, and the land had opened into a valley. He might never find shelter. To this point, the snowy wilderness had been an adventure. But in this freezing blizzard, with no barriers around him to tame the torrent of wind and snow, he might very well freeze to death before nightfall.

His mother had predicted the territories would eat him alive. *God, please don't let her be right.*

No sudden stillness split the howling wind in answer to his prayer. Nor did he feel a voice inside him giving direction on how to save himself.

But he had to do something. He couldn't stand here wishing for sunshine while his body turned to an ice block.

He turned back to Domino, stroking under his ice-encrusted forelock. The mule blinked snowy lashes at him.

"We'd best keep walking. I'd rather die doing something than standing still."

He adjusted his position to what should be straight forward on the trail between the mountains. Unless the blizzard had his senses more off-kilter than he'd thought—a deadly possibility.

Pushing off on his snowshoes, he tried to keep going in a straight line. A minute passed, but the going was slow with the wind beating against him and his spirits plunging.

He should start singing. The only song that came was that rowdy barroom tome that had played over and over from the building beside his hotel in Quebec. He'd hated the song then, but maybe today the tune could help him survive.

He forced out the lyrics to "A Lady of High Degree." The effort to move his cracked lips caused them to ache, but at least pain meant he was still alive.

Halfway through the second verse, a wooden blur appeared ahead of him. Adrien squinted, trying to discern the shape. A building?

Dragging his snowshoe-laden feet forward, he moved close enough to touch the icy surface, his thick leather gloves meeting solid wood.

A surge of energy flooded him. His imagination hadn't fooled him. He'd actually found a building.

Charging forward, he ran his hand along the rough wall as he searched for a door or other opening. The logs stretched about four strides before turning a corner. He followed them around and, finally, found the door.

Closed.

He fisted his hand and banged on it. Surely there wasn't a person living out here, so far from any fort or trading post. He'd felt like he was the only man alive for days.

The wind howling around him covered any sounds that might come from inside. No latch string hung out as a sign that visitors could enter, but surely whoever had built the cabin wouldn't mind him taking shelter from the blizzard.

He pushed his shoulder into the door. The wood wiggled as if it weren't very strong, but the barrier didn't open. He could break through with one good kick, probably.

Best try knocking first, though. Before he could raise a fist, the door swung wide.

Adrien straightened, peering into the darkness. Who had opened it?

An animal shifted inside, big and hairy. Like a bear. Or…a buffalo?

Adrien pulled Domino closer so he could reach the rifle strapped on the mule, yet he couldn't take his eyes from the creature before him. The head shifted, and a bit of pale skin appeared.

A person's face?

His breath left him in a whoosh, and he inhaled again, trying to still his thundering heart.

"What do you want?" The voice inside the fur robe yelled over the howling wind, but not even the blizzard was loud enough to disguise the high tone.

A woman?

Domino nudged his side, pulling him from the shocking discovery. He had to get them out of the wind. He jerked down the muffler that covered his mouth and inhaled to force out words.

Before he could speak, the woman swayed, first one direction, then toward the door as she clung to the wood for support.

"Are you well?" He reached out. The dim light and that dark fur shrouding her made her face seem as pale as death. He stepped forward to help her—or tried to, but his snowshoe caught on the wood transom beneath the door.

He pitched forward but caught himself on the frame.

She swayed again, and he reached out for her, but too late. Her eyes rolled back in her head, and she fell to the dirt floor.

Raising his legs high so the awkward frames cleared the doorway, he stepped inside and glanced about. Nothing moved inside the small cabin.

The place was only one dim room with a rough-built fireplace and chimney at one end. No fire in the hearth. A pile of furs lay in the corner like a sleeping pallet. That would be the best place to put her.

He pushed the door shut to block out the wind, then eased down in front of the woman and pulled the fur cape back from her face. Dark brown hair spilled over her cheek. Her skin blanched almost as white as the snow outside. He shifted her so he could find an acceptable place to put his hands to carry her.

Her closed eyelids never moved. Heavens, don't let her be dead.

She hung limp in his arms as he clomped to the stack of furs, and he tried to cradle her head in the crook of his elbow.

He sank to his knees to lay her on the low pallet, and she stirred as he pulled his hands out from under her. Thank the Lord she wasn't dead.

She didn't open her eyes, though.

"Mademoiselle." He pulled off a glove and reached to touch her forehead. A glance at his bright red fingers stilled him. His skin was so icy he may not be able to feel whether she was feverish. But maybe they'd jolt her senses enough to wake her.

He pressed his hand to her brow. His brawny skin appeared so rough and masculine next to the pale softness of her features.

Her lashes fluttered. Long, black lashes that raised to reveal a sliver of blue. Her gaze seemed sleepy as it swept in a slow arc. When her focus lifted to his face, her eyes widened, and she came to life. Her muscles tightened under his hand, and she pulled back.

He jerked away, scooting backward to give her more space. Except the snowshoes wouldn't let his feet move where he commanded. His body obeyed, however, shifting backward without anything to hold him up.

He toppled to the floor, landing on the raised edge of his snowshoe. The ache in his backside would leave a bruise tomorrow. He glanced at the woman to see if she'd caught his less-than-graceful retreat.

She lay there, rounded eyes luminous against her delicate features as she stared at him. She spoke, but the words came in English, and the only sound he could decipher was "Who."

Pushing up to a crouch, he worked his snowshoes backward to give her a bit of space. Then he focused on the woman again and spoke in his native tongue. "I only speak French. My name is Adrien Lockman."

Her brows knit in a thoughtful expression. Not complete confusion as he'd expected. Maybe she understood a bit of the language. He pressed on, keeping his words slow and as clear as he could make them with his mouth still frozen. "You are unwell. What can I get you for your relief?"

She started to sit up, but the way her face scrunched and her mouth pinched, the effort proved too difficult.

"Lie still." He wanted to reach out and ease her back down, but something about the wariness in her eyes put him in mind of a cornered wildcat. "I won't hurt you. I mean only to help. What is your name?"

She gave up trying to rise. Something must be truly wrong with her if she was that weak. Her gaze arrowed a seething glare his way. "What is your business here?" She spoke in French, although halting and stilted.

He glanced over his shoulder at the closed door, the wind still howling outside. "I grew lost in the blizzard and almost ran into your cabin. I was hoping you would shelter my mule and me until the snow stops." He ran his gaze over her face, drawn and pale. "It's good I came when I did. You are not well. What can I get for you? Water to drink? Maybe a broth? Have you any stew or meat I can simmer?"

She shook her head. "There's water by the hearth. I don't need food. Let me rest and I'll be well."

He glanced at the hearth where a pot which probably held the water sat. Then he slid his gaze around the rest of the room. Sparse. Really, there was almost nothing else there. Not even scraps of wood to build a fire. Did that mean she didn't have food either? That would certainly explain her weakened state.

Rising to his feet, he took a step back so he wouldn't tower over her. "Do you mind if I bring my mule inside? Only until the wind settles down."

She nodded. "Bring him."

Thank you, Lord. Once he had Domino settled, he'd get a fire going and heat some food for her. Beans would be warm and stick to her belly, but maybe he'd start with something quicker. He could parboil a bit of venison. She didn't look like she'd last long enough for the beans to cook without something to hold her over.

Within minutes, he had his snowshoes off and a fire licking at the dried wood he'd stored in Domino's pack. The oilskin had kept all his supplies nice and dry, despite the blizzard.

Domino let out a bray as he sniffed the interior of the cabin. If the place had a wood floor, Adrian would've hesitated to bring the animal in. But honestly, this cabin wasn't as nice as most barns back in France.

The mule shuffled forward to sniff the furs, moving toward the woman lying atop them.

She held out a gloved hand and spoke to the animal in English. Then she switched to French. "What's his name?"

Adrien glanced over. "Domino." He picked up the pot from his supplies and headed toward the door.

"Where are you going?"

He paused with his hand on the door latch and turned to look at her. She'd pulled the buffalo robe down as though prepared to launch out of the bed after him. Did she think he planned to walk out the door and not come back?

"Rest easy. I'm gathering snow to melt for water."

Her body seemed to relax into the furs, looking so tiny among them. How long had she been holed up in this cabin without food and warmth?

He turned back to the door and slipped outside. The blizzard still blew with all its fury, slamming into him as he crouched in the snow just beyond the door. He'd left his gloves off to make the work easier, and his numb hands stuck to the cast iron handles on the pot.

With all haste, he slipped back into the cabin, closed the door behind him, then barred it shut against the weather. Domino brayed again, whether to welcome him or protest the gust of wind and snow was hard to tell.

Adrien didn't look at the woman as he worked over the fire, but the burn of her gaze bore into him. Where had she come from? How had she ended up here alone? So many questions, yet they would have to wait until she'd eaten and warmed herself. Maybe then her wariness would ease.

When the snow in the pot melted and grew hot, he scooped out a cup full and turned to the woman. "Drink this to warm you."

She shrank back into the blankets, so he slowed his approach, keeping a little distance between them as he held the mug out.

That seemed to help, for she loosened her clutch on her fur covering and reached for the mug. Her hand trembled, making him hesitate to release the cup into her grasp.

"Here, I'll help hold it while you drink."

Her gaze flew to his face, the wary look turning to full suspicion. What did she think he would do? Dump the hot liquid on her?

He forced his expression to gentle even more. "Just until you get warm. The water is hot, we wouldn't want it to slosh on you."

Her hard expression softened a touch, and she focused on the cup and gripped the handle.

Together, they eased the mug to her lips and she sipped. Her face scrunched as the water went down, probably because of the warmth.

The liquid shouldn't be hot enough to scald her, but she must have been frozen through.

Her next swallow was less hesitant, and she started to drink hungrily. When she'd gulped down half the mug, he eased it away.

"Let that settle a bit, then have more."

She sank back onto the pallet, her face more relaxed, lashes sinking lower so her blue eyes were hooded in their shadows. She would probably need a few moments for the hot liquid to work its magic and thaw her from the inside out.

At least she was on her way.

He turned back to the water over the fire, now boiling and ready to accept the venison. Once he got some food into her, he had more than a few questions. Where were they? How had she ended up with no food or warmth?

And the question that loomed strongest in his mind—who was this woman?

CHAPTER 2

This life is a battle I almost grow too tired to fight. But for one thing that
drives me onward.
~ Mary

Mary Standish eyed the man kneeling beside her fireplace. Who was he and where had he come from? Or, the real question, could he be trusted? She'd not seen a human since her husband, Thomas, died more than three months ago, rest his soul. People didn't come this far into the mountain country during winter. At least, white men didn't. Even the Indians had been smart enough to foresee this awful season and most had headed south.

If only she hadn't been too stubborn to accompany them. South or east. She'd have to go sooner or later now that she was alone, but she'd hoped for one more peaceful winter before rejoining civilization.

She hadn't expected it to be the fiercest cold she'd ever experienced. Even the animals had all shifted southward, leaving her with dwindling food and less strength by the day.

And now, just when another blizzard struck to keep her from finding food, this man and his mule appeared out of nowhere.

He turned to her with a trencher in his hand. "I have beans cooking, but this venison will hold you over."

She had to work hard to translate his French words. His tone was smooth and his manner unhurried, which made it easier. Thank the Lord for that winter she and Thomas had spent with the French trappers. She'd learned to understand almost everything they said, although she stumbled over her words when she tried to speak back to them.

The man, Adrian Lockman, knelt beside her bed, the wooden plate in hand. She fought the urge to pull away from him. In truth, her body wasn't obeying much she asked of it today. Every inch of movement required so much energy, and she needed to conserve what she could for the life growing inside her.

She'd take the food he offered. As much for the babe as for herself. Then, as soon as she was strong enough to stand and the wind died down, she'd send him on his way—at gunpoint if she had to. She needed her only remaining rifle bullet in case she found an animal large enough to feed her the rest of the winter. But if this man tried to take advantage of her, alone as they were in this mountain wilderness, she'd not hesitate to use it on him.

Mary kept her gaze on the man's face while she took meat from the plate. Her midsection issued a rather loud growl as the scent of the food wafted through her. The meat tasted salty, and gamey, and better than anything she'd eaten in her life. She chewed the first bite only a little before letting it slide down to silence her eager middle.

The little bit of meat was gone long before her stomach stopped gurgling, and the tempting aroma of beans cooking didn't help matters.

Mr. Lockman had been moving around the little cabin while she ate, mostly working with the packs he'd unloaded from his mule. He'd fed the animal something on the floor of her house, probably not the cleanest of activities for a dwelling. Funny, she hadn't thought twice when he'd first brought the mule into the cabin, what with the blowing cold outside.

Not that this was much of a home. She and Thomas had built the place a few years back and she hadn't spent much time there since. At least, not until he died. It seemed as if her life had lost some of its meaning when that bear knocked him over with a massive paw.

Their dreams had started as Thomas's dreams, but she hadn't minded. Anything to get her away from stuffy city life and the people who always mocked her. She'd been happy to marry a man much older and ride off to the mountain wilderness. They'd become trappers and traders for the Hudson Bay Company—one adventure after another.

But the fun in their four-year journey had died with Thomas. And now, she'd almost resigned herself to following his demise. Not that she'd die of a broken heart, but from this merciless winter. Alas, that choice wouldn't be fair to their little one. If she had any chance of making it to spring, she had to try.

The mule let out a bray that rose loudly over the wind howling outside, and she reached a gloved hand to the animal. "Hey, Domino. Here, boy."

He shuffled toward her, leading with his nose as he sniffed up her buffalo robe covering. He finally reached her fingers, and she stroked the thick winter hair on his jaw.

"Thatta boy." She scratched under his neck, and the mule stretched out as though relishing the attention.

"He'll be your friend always."

Mary tried not to jump at the sound of the man's voice. She'd been on her own far too long.

She looked over at him as he pulled a bundle from his pack. "What are you doing here, Mr. Lockman?"

He raised dark brows at her, then turned his focus to unwrapping his bundle. "I told you. I was lost in the storm and ran into your cabin. Domino and I were pleased to find you. We thought we would freeze out there when the blizzard grew so thick." He pulled the cloth away from his parcel—a satchel of some kind, like what was used to package food—then looked up to meet her gaze. "May I ask your name, Mademoiselle?"

She stiffened. Should she withhold her name? There didn't seem to be a reason to keep it from him, although sharing her name felt like a welcome she didn't want to offer. Still, she would do best to get along with him until she was stronger. "Madame Mary Standish."

His eyes widened for a second—probably by the married status implied by the word *Madame*. Something else flickered through his eyes before he dropped his gaze back to the sack in his hands. "How long have you been holed up in this cabin?"

"A while." That wasn't any of his business.

The mule inched closer, giving her access to stroke his neck through the thick winter hair. Thankfully, his master didn't push any further, and they were left with the crackling of the fire and the sound of the blizzard outside.

And the aroma of those cooking beans. She could practically taste them, her muscles seeming to grow stronger from just imagining how smoothly they would go down.

At long last—when she had almost decided to climb out from the furs and scoop a helping of beans herself—Mr. Lockman ambled over to the pot and raised up a ladle full of food.

"I'm sure they're ready by now." *Oh, half-pence.* She hadn't meant to say that. Her stomach must have clamped a hand over her good sense and blurted the words.

He slid a glance her way, and the corners of his mouth twitched. Yet, his eyes didn't twinkle, and the lack of sparkle shrouded the hint of a smile with sadness. After reaching for the trencher, he ladled a heaping portion. "*Oui.* I agree. The beans may be crunchy, but they'll be warm and filling."

Crunchy she could handle much better than this out-of-control feeling from the growing babe within that made her mouth and body take possession of her mind.

She gulped the beans faster than she should have. Her mother and sister back in Baltimore would have been appalled at her lack of decorum. But they'd never been half-starved and half-frozen. Besides, she'd long stopped caring what her family thought of her actions, and survival was more important than their good opinion now.

When every scrap of food had been scooped from her trencher, she lowered the dish. She had a mind to lick the juice clean, but that was probably going too far. The pinching in her midsection eased. Or rather, turned to an unsettled roiling. Perhaps she shouldn't have eaten so quickly.

"Something to drink?" Mr. Lockman held out the tin cup, and she reached for it. Her hand no longer shook.

The tepid water seeped down her throat, soothing the raw places and settling the turmoil in her stomach.

She breathed out a long breath and lowered the mug. Better. Much better.

The Frenchman knelt by the fire, watching her. Although her strength seemed to be coming back with every minute that passed, she still didn't quite have the pluck to face him. Not with the steel resolve she needed to send him on his way.

So she settled for a simple statement. "Thank you for the food." She owed him that. Now that she'd eaten a decent meal, as soon as the snow subsided, she'd check her traps. She'd been given a second chance.

She just had to keep the baby and herself alive for the rest of the winter.

Then she could get on with her life. But what kind of life, and where would that be?

❧

"I'll bed down in this corner for the night." Adrien pointed to the side of the fireplace opposite Madame Standish.

Her gaze seared him, but he didn't dare meet it head-on. Surely she didn't think he'd leave with dark coming on just because the wind and snow had died down. He wouldn't be abandoning her in the morning either, not until he had a good supply of meat and firewood stored up for her. He'd seen too much death in his life. No woman

14

would freeze or starve on his watch, not even in this wild Canadian territory.

After he spread out his bedroll and checked Domino one last time, he crouched by the fire to add a few more logs. "This is the last of the firewood I brought with me, so it might be cold by morning. Stay in your furs and I'll gather wood first thing. When it warms tomorrow, I'll do some hunting. I have plenty of food for breakfast though, so don't worry."

An indignant sound came from the direction of the woman, and he turned to look at her as she raised herself up to a sitting position. At least she was stronger now. Strong enough for those blue eyes to shoot arrows at him. "You have no need to stay here on my account, Monsieur Lockman. I'll be up before you in the morning and will gather my own firewood and meat."

She was feisty, now that she'd had a bit to eat. But her face still shone pale in the dim light. She needed more rest, warmth, and good food before she went to battle—with him or the elements. He'd do best not to ruffle her.

He nodded. "We'll see how things go in the morning."

She didn't answer aloud, but the burn of her gaze followed him as he moved toward his blankets and settled in.

At last, she sank back onto her pallet, and silence stretched over them thicker than the snow outside. The crackle and popping of the fire grew louder, making him even more aware of the woman lying across the room.

He turned onto his side away from her. He was weary enough that sleep should come soon. Tomorrow, he'd have his work cut out for him, helping this woman who didn't seem to want him around.

CHAPTER 3

I don't always understand Your ways, oh God. Yet I am willing.
~ Adrien's Journal

That was the best night's sleep Mary'd had in months. She stretched under the worn fur coverings, relishing in the morning's glow and the warmth that seeped around her. The fire crackled in the hearth, hot coals glowing red. Which meant it'd been rekindled hours before.

She let her arms sink back under the covers as the realities from the day before formed clear images in her mind. Where had Mr. Lockman gone? He'd obviously done much this morning, considering the warm cabin and roaring fire. He must have been up early to gather wood, then bring it back to dry out. Hadn't she told him she'd do all that? But with the warmth soothing her aching bones, she couldn't quite be angry with him.

And now where was he? A glance at the corner where he'd slept showed the space clean except for the supplies he'd taken off his mule's pack. Wherever he'd gone, he must have taken poor Domino with him.

Mary folded the pelts back and pushed herself upright, then shifted her feet to the floor. She could even feel her toes inside her boots. It was a wonder they hadn't frozen stiff and fallen off after she'd run out of firewood. God had shown her mercy, for whatever reason. Or maybe Adrien's arrival had simply been a stroke of luck.

She eased up to a standing position, then braced a hand against the wall to keep herself upright as the room swirled around her. She shouldn't still be this weak. Finally, her vision cleared some, and she shuffled toward the fireplace. The pot of beans sat on the stones, out of the reach of the flame but in a position where they would stay warm.

Perhaps she should feel guilty for eating the stranger's food, but she'd replenish his supplies as soon as she could get out to check her traps. For now, the baby needed sustenance to grow inside her.

Lockman had rinsed the trencher and placed it with the other utensils on a corner of the hearth. She scooped a heaping portion and perched on the edge of the hearth, then set into the food.

After the first couple of bites, her stomach began the same roiling it had taken up the night before, so she forced herself to slow and enjoy the food. He'd put bits of meat in with the beans, giving them a richer taste.

Even eating slowly, the helping of beans was gone before her stomach felt full. She eyed what remained in the pot—at least two more servings. They should conserve the food, though. Even if Lockman had gone to hunt as he'd said he would, there was a chance he wouldn't find game in this tundra. All the smart animals had moved south.

They would need those leftover beans for a meal, either tonight or tomorrow. Unless she could get out to check her traps.

She forced her weary muscles to lift her to her feet, then carried the used dishes toward the door. The latch-string was draped outside so Lockman could come in when he returned, one more sign he *had* planned to return.

As she opened the door, a gust of icy wind slammed into her face, obliterating the warm peace in the room. She stepped outside, pulling her cloak tight around her, and secured the door. The fur seemed thin and flimsy against the bitter cold, but at least the blizzard had ceased. Her feet sank into the snow until it rose above her knees, and she could see the snowshoe tracks and deeper hoof marks where Lockman and his mule had set off. They'd headed toward a patch of trees on the far side of the lake. He'd have as much luck finding game there as anywhere.

Maybe she should go after him. Help, if he needed it, and check her traps. But she shucked the idea as soon as it came, dropping to her haunches at a clean patch of snow to wipe the dishes clean.

After finishing her work outside, she slipped back into the cabin, her teeth chattering violently as she shut the door and moved back to the fire. She'd have to force herself to take action soon, but a few more minutes of this blessed warmth wouldn't hurt. Surely.

She set the dishes back on the hearth, then allowed her gaze to wander to the packs on the floor by the far wall. What did the man carry in his supplies? Just food and basic necessities? Was he a trapper for Hudson Bay? That was one of the few reasons she could imagine a white man coming out here in the dead of winter. At least, one of the few upstanding reasons. If he were a murderer escaping punishment, this would be the perfect place to hide.

Maybe a look inside those packs would give her a clue about his business.

She glanced at the door as if it could tell her whether Lockman would return soon. Only the crackle of the fire and the wind outside broke the silence. She crept toward the packs. There were two large leather satchels and three smaller bundles wrapped in cloth. Those were likely clothing, so she focused on the leather bags. They were both tied shut with drawstring openings.

It didn't take long for her to open the first, which appeared to hold food supplies. Smaller bags of cornmeal, strips of meat, and other staples. Her midsection gurgled, either from the sight of food or the aromas wafting from the bag. It looked as if they wouldn't be going hungry for a while.

Or rather...*he* wouldn't. Because she'd send him on his way as soon as he returned from his hunting excursion.

After retying the first sack closed, she moved to the second. This looked to be his catch-all, with miscellaneous straps and small bundles and even a couple of books. She pulled out the leather-bound volumes. *La Bible* was printed across one in fading lettering. The ragged corners of that book bespoke many hours of reading—either that or it had rambled around the pack far too long. Either way, the fact that he owned a Bible and considered it dear enough to haul all the way through the Canadian territory said something for his character.

Mayhap he wasn't a murderer. Or if so, perhaps he'd chosen reform.

The other book held no title, and a flip through the pages revealed small French script. A ledger of some kind? She squinted to decipher the foreign writing. It appeared to be a journal, its entries dated.

She closed the book, forcing down her curiosity. She'd snooped enough without reading his personal logbook. But she did pause and allow her gloved finger to trace the cover. A rich leather. Either he'd once possessed no shortage of money or he took pride in a quality book.

Whichever the case, a different picture was forming in her mind of this man who'd appeared on her doorstep. Yet her questions remained. Who was this Adrien Lockman, and why had he come?

$\sim$

*A*drien rapped on the rickety door of the ramshackle cabin and waited. He'd been gone much longer than planned, but everything seemed to take much more time than it should on these snowshoes. And the hunting had been scarcer than he'd expected. He'd finally seen a red fox darting through the trees near the shelter he'd made for Domino.

The wind whipped between his hood and neck, and he hunched lower against the chill. If the latch string were out the way he'd left it, he'd go on in. Perhaps this was a sign from Madame Standish that she didn't welcome his help. Although why she wanted him to leave so strongly, he didn't understand. She might be dead by now if he hadn't shown up yesterday.

The door opened with a whoosh, and he stepped in, away from the bitter cold. The warmth of the small room sank over him like a thick blanket.

"I wasn't sure you'd come back."

He glanced at Madame Standish as she closed the door. She wore a fur cloak, but the hood was lowered so he could see her face clearly for the first time. She was a striking woman, especially with those intense blue eyes. Perhaps it was the gauntness of her face that made them stand out so much.

Forcing himself to look away, he carried his load of logs to the fireplace and dropped them beside it. Then he laid his other bundle on the hearth. "I finally found a fox for the evening meal. I don't have a gridiron, so it might be easiest to cut the meat in strips and roast each piece on a rod. I have a little corn meal if you want something to hold you over."

He turned to look back at her. "I should have left it out in case you finished the beans and were still hungry."

Her gaze flicked to the pot he'd left beside the fire, and her face seemed uncertain. She had finished the beans, hadn't she?

Leaning closer, he peered into the dish. Two helpings were still in there. A surge of heat rushed up his chest, and he turned to glare at the woman. "Why didn't you eat more? There's plenty there."

She raised her chin, her blue eyes flashing dark. "I did eat. Besides, I don't need your food, Monsieur Lockman. I appreciate the help you gave yesterday, but I'm much improved, and you don't need to concern yourself with me any longer."

He turned back to face the fire, taking in slow deep breaths to still the frustration coursing through his veins. Why did she resist his help so much? All he wanted was to provide food, for mercy's sake. It wasn't as if he planned a slow torture.

Perhaps the presence of a man in her cabin made her nervous. He had marched in and taken over, after all. Of course, she'd been unconscious for part of it, so he'd had to do what was necessary to keep her alive.

Maybe she'd been away from civilization for so long, it would take her a while to warm up to him. He'd just have to show a bit of patience.

As he built up the fire again, then sliced the meat and set chunks to roast, he could feel the woman's presence behind him. She was moving about, but it wasn't the sounds of her shuffling that told him where she was. In truth, she was so quiet, he almost couldn't hear her movements.

But he could feel them. Like the warmth of the sun on a French summer day, her presence seemed to penetrate the thickness of his coat and seer his skin. What was she doing back there?

The cabin didn't hold a stick of furniture, so it wasn't likely she was cleaning. Only a few pieces of clothing or what-nots hung from nails and pegs on the walls. She must use the rock hearth as a table to prepare food the way he was doing—when she had food to prepare, anyway.

With the food cooking, he rose to his feet and pulled his gloves back on. "I have more firewood stacked out by the trees. I'm going to go bring it inside so it will dry out."

The woman straightened from where she rifled for something in a satchel. "I can help carry."

He scanned her. She appeared steady on her feet now, although he'd feel better if she ate another scoop of beans before heading out into the elements. But she was already moving toward the door, pulling her cape tight around her as she went. She lifted a pair of snowshoes from the wall and stooped to lace them on.

She might end up making the trip harder for him, but maybe if he allowed her to work alongside him, she'd see he wasn't such a scoundrel.

They trekked across the snow, following his earlier tracks to where he'd settled Domino and left the wood. The walk would have taken five minutes if he'd gone alone, but they were moving slower this time.

Madame Standish had a sure stride, as if she'd marched many miles on snowshoes. But her legs were shorter than his, and her breaths sounded hoarse in the icy air. He forced himself to take short steps and walk slower than his normal lanky stride.

Finally, they reached the woods, and Domino met them with a bray from under the branch shelter Adrien had made. Madame walked to him first and took the mule's head in her arms, stroking his jaw and neck as she spoke in soft murmurings.

The mule relished every word and touch, and it wasn't hard to wonder why. To have such a pretty lady lavish that much attention was a treat neither he nor the mule had experienced in a month of Tuesdays.

After a few moments, she turned and sent him an expectant look. "You have the wood stacked?"

He jerked into action. He shouldn't be just standing there, ogling her and wishing he were the mule.

Motioning toward the logs, he let her gather her load first. Then he piled as much as he could carry into his arms and set off in her tracks.

CHAPTER 4

Many things I have learned, yet what I don't know still haunts me.
~ Mary

The trek to gather wood had been just what Mary needed to invigorate her senses. Although it had winded her more than the simple hike should have.

She took over preparations of the food, dishing out the meat and leftover beans on the two trenchers Thomas had carved their first winter in the mountains.

Lockman took the dish she handed him and settled cross-legged beside the hearth. "It looks good enough to eat." He raised his platter as if in toast and gave her a grin that showed smile lines at the corners of his eyes and even, white teeth.

Maybe it was the fact she hadn't seen a grin like that in months, but his look raised a flutter in her chest. She dropped her gaze to her food. "Where are you headed from here, Monsieur Lockman?" That would be a better path for her thoughts.

"I'd planned to travel northwest, as far as I can go in a month's time. Then I'll come back and settle in a valley I found about a week ago."

She jerked her head up. "A valley? Where?" She knew where he meant, even without asking. Anyone who laid eyes on the wide stretch of land a couple day's ride to the east would long for a home there. Thomas had entertained notions of it, but he'd not been the type to settle down. Certainly not with a ranch and all its responsibilities that would tie him in one place.

Lockman motioned toward the east. "It was about five days' walk, through a narrow trail between the mountains."

That was the one.

She studied him, with his dark eyes and black hair. He had the look of a Frenchman, no doubt. His eyes held a touch of sparkle, and he seemed to always have those faint creases at the corners. Maybe she noticed it now because they lit with an inner enthusiasm. She knew that enthusiasm, had felt it when she'd first seen that stretch of valley four years ago.

But she'd let her dream die as she realized it would never come to pass. And now, she kept her expression impassive as she took another bite of beans.

"And what of you, Madame Standish? Were you from the Canadas before coming out here?"

Should she tell him anything? She had nothing to hide. He'd already realized she was here alone, so nothing else about her could lead to danger. She loaded beans onto a slab of meat. "I grew up in the States. Maryland. Came up here after I married."

"Really? How long ago was that?" He was the curious type, for sure.

"About four years." She took another bite, intentionally not looking at him.

"So you've lived in these mountains four years? What did your husband do to earn your living?" He spoke in the past tense, as though he knew Thomas had passed. But of course he would think her widowed. She'd given him her married name, and no decent husband would leave his wife to die in a blizzard if he could help it. Anyone would assume the man must be deceased.

"We trapped for the Hudson Bay Company." She took a sip of the water she'd melted earlier from snow.

"Is your husband…?" And there came the question.

Should she answer him? Remove any doubt that she was alone with no one who might return for her? Maybe not just yet.

So she pretended to understand the question a different way. "We worked together. Took turns checking the traps and working the hides. Thomas handled the bartering, and I did most of the cooking. A decent living."

He didn't respond, but she could feel the questions that must be churning in his mind. How had she gone from the life she described to fainting on her own doorstep, starving and half-frozen? That wasn't a tale she was ready to offer just yet.

"And what of you? You're from Old France?" She eyed him, watching for signs he might cover up something in his story.

A look of amusement flickered through his eyes. "I am. And I am pleased you can tell me apart from these Canadian ruffians." He paused as if waiting for her to explain how she knew his home country.

She shrugged. "It was a guess. Most French Canadians speak at least a little English. And the way you pronounce things is a bit different than I learned."

He leaned forward. "And how is it you know my language? You speak it well for an American."

She poked at her food, letting the memories filter back through her. "We wintered in a little fort a couple years ago. Most of the men there were *Voyageurs* from Montreal. They only spoke a little English, so we learned French. They would sit at night and tell story after story about their travels and the trading with the Indians."

"I can only imagine the tales. I saw a few Indians at the forts on my way here. They appeared to be a regal sort of people, but the stories I've heard make them sound savage."

The image of one of the women from the fort slipped into her mind, bringing a smile. "Their ways were different, but I never thought of them as savage. One of the trappers married a woman from the Ojibwa tribe. I never could pronounce her Indian name, so I called her Neengay like some of the others called her. She was the daughter of a great chief and did a lot of the trading with her husband. What she accomplished was exceptional."

She glanced up at him, meeting his curious gaze. "But you didn't finish telling me of your background, Monsieur Lockman. Why is it you came across the ocean?"

He nodded. "My apologies. France has become so…" He seemed to struggle for the right word. "There is much political turmoil. Everyone seeking power and willing to stop at nothing to obtain it. I was nearly caught up in another rebellion last summer and finally decided there must be a better place. A place without corrupt governments and constant uprisings.

"So, I boarded a ship for the Canadas and landed in Québec. I had thought to stay there, but the place reminded me too much of Paris, only less civilized. I boarded another boat to take me down the Ottawa River, then kept moving farther inland. I found Domino at one of the forts and knew he was meant to be my companion." He had that look in his eye, the thirst for adventure she'd first seen in Thomas. That look could be contagious, she knew from experience. Yet it felt different on this man.

She forced herself to push aside those thoughts. "You have no family that would hold you to France?"

"Only a mother, but she's been comfortably settled with my uncle and his family for many years now. She did not wish to leave her life there."

No father? No wife and children? Perhaps that would be prying too far to ask.

She took another bite of meat, and silence settled over them as they ate. Each bite held such flavor, she almost closed her eyes to relish the taste.

As she scooped the last of the beans from her trencher, Lockman rose and moved toward the fire. He grabbed one of the last chunks of meat and turned to her, then placed it on her plate.

"Oh...no." She tried to pull her tray back. "We should save that. You'll need to take provisions with you."

But he'd already dumped the food and returned to his seat, focusing on the trencher in front of him. "You need to eat to regain your strength. I've saved a lot of the meat for us tomorrow. What I cooked tonight is to be eaten tonight."

He finally looked up at her, a defiant set to his jaw.

Well, she could be more stubborn than he. She lowered her trencher to her lap. "I'll go out tomorrow and check my traps. They'll provide me plenty of food for weeks to come."

"That's good. So you should eat up now to prepare your strength for that trek tomorrow."

She squared her shoulders to fight back, but the words *prepare your strength* found home somewhere deep in her chest. It wasn't her strength she had to worry about, it was the little one inside her. If the child had survived her near starvation, this little fighter needed all the strength she could give him.

She reached for the meat and took a bite.

~

The next morning didn't dawn, it blew in with an icy fury. Adrien listened to the wind attack the cabin as he lay in his bedroll. Would the structure withstand the gusts, each seeming more intent on destruction than the one before? No doubt there was snow blowing on that wind, thick enough to block one's vision.

At least Madame Standish wouldn't expect him to leave first thing this morning, as she'd suggested the night before. She wouldn't be able to check her traps as she'd planned either. It was a good thing he'd saved meat from that fox and still had a few supplies in his pack. He was starting to see how this weather could have driven her to the point where she had no food or firewood left.

He pushed his covers aside and sat up. A movement rustled on the pallet across the room, but he forced himself not to look there. He should probably hang a blanket to allow her more privacy. Later today, he'd get it done. There likely wouldn't be much to occupy him if the weather was as bad as he imagined.

After stoking the fire, he bundled himself and took the pot outside. He could attend to personal matters, then gather clean snow to melt for breakfast.

He had corncake batter ready to scoop into circles by the time Madame Standish sat up on her pallet. The fire seemed to heat his face twice over as her gaze tracked his movements. What did she think of him? Based on her wariness, perhaps he didn't want to know.

Still, surely he'd proven he didn't plan to take advantage of her. Surely her suspicions were beginning to wane. Or maybe he needed to do more to convince her. Hanging the blanket to allow her privacy might be a step. He'd have to look for more ways, too.

For now, he allowed himself to glance her way. "Good morning. Sleep well?"

She nodded. Once again, she'd slept in her clothes and coat. In fact, he'd never seen her without the outerwear bundling her tight. But above the furskin coat, her face held a sleepy look that tightened his chest. Her rumpled hair had pulled loose from her braid, giving her a look of innocence that showed just how young she must be. Five and twenty? Maybe even younger.

And she'd been left to fend for herself in this massive wilderness. She'd not said what happened to her husband, but he could only assume the man had died. Had Monsieur Standish ever considered what would happen to this beautiful woman he left behind?

Her gaze wandered up to the rafters as another gust of wind howled through the space between the logs. He used the interruption to turn back to his work with the food.

"It sounds like another blizzard is here." The sigh in her voice was plain.

"It's not as bad as the other day. Only a little snow falling, and you can still see decently far." He scooped a final circle of batter into the pot and positioned it in the fire near the thickest coals.

"For now. It'll get worse before the day's over." She rose and straightened her fur coverings, then moved toward the door, probably to attend to her morning ministrations.

She might be right about the blizzard. Which meant he needed to gather enough wood early, while he still could. As soon as they'd both eaten, he'd get moving.

The corncakes cooked slowly since the fire was still regaining warmth, yet Madame Standish hadn't returned by the time he scooped the second batch of cakes out of the pan.

Had the snowfall turned to a blizzard? Could she not find her way back to the cabin? Or maybe she'd been attacked by a wild animal starving from the intense winter.

After setting the plate of corn cakes on the corner of the hearth, he grabbed his gloves and pushed to his feet. Something wasn't right. The woman might need him.

He scooped up his rifle on his way outside, then hung the latch string over the door as he closed it. The leather strip flapped as the wind gusted. He pulled his fur cap lower over his head and ears, then tugged his coat higher so the wind couldn't slip under it.

A scan of the snow around them showed no sign of tracks, neither his nor Madame Standish's. The wind and blowing snow must have obliterated them, leaving him no hint of where the woman had gone.

There was no movement around the lake in the far distance, nor the mountain ranges on either side of the cabin. So, he strode around to check behind the building.

She wasn't there either. The blowing snow cloaked the distant mountains with a fog-like haze, but he could still make out the V in the cliffs that formed the gap he'd traveled through to get here. And a little farther to the right, the trees where he'd been gathering wood and made the shelter for Domino. Had she gone to check the mule?

He'd travel faster with snowshoes, but they took so long to lace on, he might reach the trees just as quickly without. And he didn't have the patience for them right now.

Clutching his rifle in one hand, he started through the knee-high snow. Why hadn't she said she was leaving before traipsing off?

A few minutes into the journey, he was huffing from struggling through the icy snow, the bitter air searing his lungs with each inhale. He should have grabbed his muffler to shield his face. He paused to catch his breath and check for any sign of the woman. The trees still looked to be at least as far away as he'd traveled.

He raised his hands to cup his mouth and called out, "Madame Standish!" His words tried to stretch across the expanse, but the wind and snow seemed to soak them in.

He had to reach those trees. Surely she would be there.

If not... Well, he couldn't imagine what he'd do if not.

CHAPTER 5

My heart yearns to accomplish this task entrusted to me. Yet why must it be
so hard? Or should I say...hard-headed.
~ Adrien's Journal

"Come, boy. It's for your good." Mary stroked the mule's head, then reached for the lead rope again and tugged. "Let's go."

Domino didn't budge from the edge of the woods. She didn't blame him—the snow swirling past the trees was much worse than under this canopy. But since the wind blew down the shelter Lockman had made for him, the mule would be much better off if she moved him to the cave hidden within the far mountain.

But getting him to that shelter required stepping out into the barrage of wind and ice.

She paused to stroke the mule on the center of his forehead. She'd had a bit of experience with mules, mostly with a couple belonging to those French trappers. They earned their reputation for stubbornness honestly. But a mule would usually oblige anything you asked if you said it with a gentle tone and a kind stroke.

When she tugged on the rope this time, Domino did move one hoof forward, then braced all four. Again.

She let out a long sigh and turned to look out at the weather once more. A dark spot in the snow snagged her attention, and she squinted. A person.

Adrien Lockman.

He must have wondered at her being gone so long. She hadn't actually intended to move the mule to a different spot, but when she stepped around to the back of the cabin to attend to morning matters, this patch of trees had seemed to summon her. Domino would need attention before the storm reached its peak today.

She grabbed the mule's halter again and coaxed him forward. "Walk on. If you don't come with me, you'll have to go with him."

The mule didn't budge at her words, and it took several more minutes before she had him out of the woods. When he met the biting wind, he seemed to give in to his fate and trudge forward with her. By then, Lockman was a dozen strides away.

"What are you doing?" His tone held a bite that even the wind couldn't disguise.

"Moving your animal to a better shelter. What you built has collapsed." His shelter might have been constructed well, but this wind attacked with a fury not easily withstood.

He reached her and took the rope. "I could have moved him. I'd planned to come and care for my friend after we broke our fast." His tone had softened, held a gentleness even. As close as he was, with his hard breaths fogging the air around them, his presence enveloped her.

Perhaps that was why she gave over the rope willingly. "There's a cave in the mountains across the valley. He'll be sheltered there."

He nodded. "I'll take him. Go back to the cabin and eat. The food is ready."

She fought the way her nerves bristled at his dismissal. "You don't know where to go. I'll take him. You can gather firewood from these trees." He had to see the wisdom in her plan.

And he seemed to. His expression turned grim, but he handed the mule's rope back to her. Then he patted the animal's neck. "Go with her, friend."

The mule must have understood his words, for he stepped forward the first time she asked. As if all he needed was his owner's approval. Finicky animal.

The snowfall looked to be growing thicker as she led the mule past the cabin. She was tempted to stop in and warm herself. Or grab some of the food Lockman had said was waiting. But she needed to settle Domino in his new shelter quickly, then get back before the snow and wind made it hard to find her way. She knew this valley intimately, yet she'd experienced the way a blizzard could strip her of all sense of direction.

She and the mule trudged a few more achingly cold minutes, then a shout behind her brought her up short. Lockman?

Yes, through the haze of white, a dark figure bobbed through the snow toward them. What was he doing now?

He panted as he reached them, his shoulders heaving in his struggle to draw breath. His dark beard didn't cover the red splotches of cold on his cheeks and nose.

"What is it?" Her pulse lurched in her neck. What could have sent him running to catch her?

"I'll go." His words were almost impossible to interpret through his gasping French.

She waited for him to catch his breath and finish the sentence, but it didn't look as though he planned to speak again. Finally, she prompted, "Go where?"

He reached for the mule's rope. "I'll take him. You go to the cabin."

She almost growled as meaning sank through her. Hadn't they been through this already? "Lockman, I said I'll take him. Didn't you get the firewood?" If he'd walked all the way back here without a load of wood, he was half-witted enough to have his head knocked.

"I brought the wood. But the weather is turning bad now. You need to go in where you'll be safe." He gripped the rope and tried to pull it from her hands.

She ignored his effort, but held tight and started walking. He was being ridiculous now, but he would see that when she set her mind to something, she accomplished it. Besides, it would be foolish to send him to look for the cave in this weather. "You'll never find the cave. I'm going myself. I'll return posthaste."

He called an answer above the wind, and she didn't turn to look at him around the edge of her hood. Just kept marching through the snow toward the far mountains. With the weather worsening by the minute, they had no time for foolishness.

~

Such foolishness would get her killed.

Adrien marched behind the woman as he struggled to catch his breath. His lungs burned from inhaling deep drafts of the icy air, but he was still stronger than she at this point.

And he had the rope he'd grabbed at the cabin when he dumped the load of sticks. If the blizzard grew severe before they returned, they'd need more than rope, but maybe it would help. Maybe. Anyway, it had been lying there and seemed an easy thing to grab as he sprinted after the woman.

She was a stubborn one. Poor Domino would have been quite happy sharing their cabin again through this storm, although he could imagine why she wouldn't want that. Still, taking the mule to a cave for shelter wasn't worth losing her life in a blizzard. And he'd seen how quickly a blizzard could develop in this valley.

It appeared all he could do to protect her now was to follow and be there when she needed him.

The trail soon became rocky, as evidenced by the snow-covered stones he kicked as he lifted his legs high to maneuver through the accumulation.

Madame Standish went down to her knees just in front of him, and he sprinted forward to help her up. She'd already bounced back to her feet when he reached her.

"Are you all right?" He gripped her elbow to help her regain her balance, but she jerked her arm away from him, turning a fiery gaze on him.

"I'm fine." She snapped the words, but something in her gaze wavered, as though she were struggling to keep the angry mask in place. Was she afraid of him? Is that why she jerked at his touch?

He stepped back to allow her space. "Be careful. The rocks make the ground uneven." He tried to infuse a gentle tone in his voice. He meant no harm. No disrespect. How could he make her see she didn't need to fear him?

They moved slower as the ground sloped upward. The snow was blowing thicker, allowing them visibility for only a few strides ahead.

At last, the dark surface of a mountainside appeared through the white. Madame Standish slowed, then stopped when she reached the wall. She extended her hand to touch the stone surface, as though to feel whether it was quite real.

They wouldn't be going through that rock.

He scanned the cliffside in each direction, but both looked the same. What he could see through the blowing snow, anyway. "Which way?"

She looked to be contemplating. If they chose the wrong direction, they could possibly be out here for hours longer than necessary. And who knew what would happen in that time?

She pointed left. "I think this is it. But maybe we should split up."

"No." He stepped closer to her side. "How would we let the other know when we found the cave? Besides, the blizzard is too bad. It could be deadly if we separate."

She nodded, or it looked like she did. "This way then." At least she didn't argue. She must feel a little of the fear churning in his gut. They might have to stay in the cave with Domino until the wind died down. How would they keep warm? And what of food? Neither of them had broken their fast that morning, and she must be weak still from near-starving.

With her leading the mule and him walking just behind her, his hand on Domino's back, they followed the wall of mountain on their right. Minutes stretched into a quarter hour at least. The rocky surface changed to a steep, snow-covered slope, then again to the sheer wall of a cliff. Yet no cave opening.

"Does this still seem like the right direction?" He shouldn't question her, but something inside needed to know she had faith in where she was leading them.

"Shouldn't be much farther."

He burrowed deeper in his coat as a gust of wind and snow tried to attack his neck. He'd long since lost feeling in his hands and feet. Panic weaved its way through his chest, circling his lungs until it held them in a vise. It was the same panic he'd felt when the blizzard struck as he and Domino traveled through the gap in the mountains, just before they found the lonely log cabin.

See us, Lord. Find us in this ferocious world of ice. Save us. God had proved His faithfulness that day. Surely He'd not saved them only to let them die in the elements now.

More minutes passed with nothing but him, her, the mule, and the unending wall of rock on their right.

And then she stopped.

He raised a hand to brace himself as he ran into her icy coat.

She moved toward the rock, hunched over and peering as she shuffled forward. Then she straightened, and turned back the way they'd come. "We passed it, but it's not far."

The statement spurred a mixture of emotions inside him. *Not far.* But how had they missed it?

She ran her hand along the rock as they walked—slowly, ever so slowly. Was the opening even large enough for them to get through?

And then, just ahead, a dark spot in the rock, taller than he and just wider than the length of his arm.

"Here." Madame Standish dropped the mule's rope and poked her head into that dark spot.

He wanted to reach out and pull her back. If that narrow opening was the cave, who knew what might be hiding inside? It was on the side of a cliff that jutted out, so no wonder they hadn't seen it coming the other direction.

Her body slipped into the darkness, leaving only one arm leaning on the rock outside.

Apprehension tightened his chest as images flickered through his mind. Didn't bears sleep in caves through the winter? He'd read stories in the papers. "Wait. I'll go in and check it."

But she was gone as though pulled inside by the claws of a silent, hairy creature. He scrambled toward the opening, slipping a hand into the darkness first. His fingers met nothing inside, so he scooted one foot forward. The snow covering the ground lessened. "Madame Standish. Are you well?" The darkness inside swallowed his words in its murky depths.

"Stay there, Adrien. I'm going to check the interior."

"Stop." He had to get her back here where she'd be safe. Relatively safe, anyway. "Come back. Now."

"In a minute." Her voice drifted from farther away than before.

Anger coursed with the fear surging through his chest, and he slipped all the way into the cave. Darkness wrapped around him like an icy blanket. How did she know where to go? Surely, she was as blind in this darkness as he.

"The cave is empty. I'm coming back." Her voice sounded more distant than before, but he could now hear her footsteps on the rock floor. Moving toward him.

When they got to a place where they were both warm and settled, it would be high time he have a talk with this woman. Whether she wanted it or not, he planned to see to her protection. And if she insisted on putting herself in danger over and over, well…she had to stop. Even if she were to come through each of these perilous undertakings without harm, he'd be an old man long before his time from worrying about her.

Her steps had grown louder, almost reaching him. He should speak and let her know his position. "How far does this cave go?" His voice echoed in the silence, the thick stone blocking out almost all sound of the wind outside.

"About twenty strides." Something touched his arm and his foot at the same time, and he reached up out of reflex.

She cried out, and he barely had time to brace himself before she slammed into him.

CHAPTER 6

I must. I can. I will.

~ Mary

*A*drien clutched at her, trying to grab something that would keep them both upright. She didn't weigh more than a sapling, but the force of her fall in the deep darkness knocked him backward.

At last, he gathered his balance, but the woman was plastered against him, her body warm and pliant. "Are you hurt?"

She stiffened as though coming back to herself. She seemed to struggle to get her feet underneath her, then pushed back away from him. "I…I'm fine. I'm sorry."

Her words came in breathy spurts. If only it were lighter in this cave and he could see her face. As it was, now that his eyes were adjusting to the darkness, he could just make out the faint outline of her hood in the light filtering around the corner of the rock that concealed the cave opening.

"Are you sure you're not injured?"

He could just hear the sound of her exhale. "I'm fine. Truly. We need to get the mule out of the weather."

Domino, yes.

Madame Standish moved toward the opening, and he let her proceed to avoid another collision.

When he rounded the edge of the cave opening, she was bent close to Domino's ear, probably trying to coax him into the narrow opening. The mule wouldn't like the small entrance, but Domino usually trudged along wherever he led. They'd get him inside without too much trouble.

But when the woman tugged the rope, the mule balked. That wasn't good. She tried for a minute longer, but Domino dug his heels deeper into the snow. Adrien knew from his earlier experiences with the mule that the more Domino refused, the harder it would be to change his mind.

He stepped out into the gusting wind, and Madame Standish halted her tugging on the rope. He stroked the animal's neck. "All right, boy. You'll like it better in there than out here. You'll have to trust me on that."

He reached for the rope, and she handed it over without argument, her gaze tracking his face. With a final pat on the mule's neck, he tugged the rope and started back to the cave's entrance.

Domino hesitated, but he didn't have his knees locked like before.

"Give him a pat on his rump, please."

The woman obeyed, and Domino stepped forward. He paused at the dark opening, and peered into the interior. Did a mule's eyes have to become accustomed to the darkness, too? Probably.

"You'll like it, boy. Trust me."

Domino eased forward, one short step at a time, until finally his shoulders cleared the opening. Then he shot forward. He had to bend around the rock at the entrance, but finally he stood inside the cave. All four legs spread, sides heaving.

*M*ary stepped to the mule's side, her heart thudding in her chest almost as loudly as his labored breathing in the stillness of the cave. "That's a boy. You made it." She crooned the words as she stroked his neck. Such trust this animal had for the man who'd dragged it out into the snowy wilderness.

It had taken her at least ten minutes to get Domino out of the woods earlier, and she might never have coaxed him into this cave on her own. Yet, he followed Lockman almost without hesitation. There must be some good in the man for his animal to trust him so implicitly.

It was too bad the cave was so dim that she could only make out Lockman's outline. She would like to study him a bit more. See if she could find out his secrets. He surely had them. Every man did.

But now wasn't the time. She forced herself to focus on what should happen next. "I don't think we can make it back to the cabin now. Not until the wind settles."

"You admit you're not able to see when you're blindfolded?" His voice held a hint of amusement.

But the fact that he was laughing at her didn't make her want to laugh along. "Even I know my limits." Sometimes.

"We need to build a fire, but I didn't bring flint. Or wood."

She let out a sigh. "Nor did I. We'll have to wait it out."

"Domino will keep us warm." That teasing tone still laced his voice. It made her dislike him and want to smile, both at the same time. How could he be so upbeat while taking refuge in a cave from a blizzard? With no light, no warmth, and no food.

The memory from a few days ago slipped back over her, weakening her muscles as that gnawing hunger nipped at her insides. She needed to sit before her legs crumpled.

Extending her hand, she shuffled toward the wall behind her. Something to lean against so she wasn't stepped on by man or beast.

"What are you doing?" Lockman's voice had lost all hint of humor.

Dizziness washed over her, or maybe just a lightness in her head.

She had to take hold of herself. Her hand pressed against cold stone, and she eased down to sit against the wall.

"Madame Standish, what's wrong?"

She almost couldn't decipher the thick French of his words. She drew in a long slow breath, held it for a beat, then let it out.

A hand touched her arm, and her heart nearly jumped out of her chest.

"What is it? Madame, what's wrong?"

She had to pull herself together and answer the man. Another breath out. "I'm fine. Just...had to sit for a moment."

His hand didn't move from her arm, but shuffling sounded on the stone floor as he eased down beside her. "Are you hungry?"

She should tell him no. It wasn't as if acknowledging her hunger would magically produce food. "Yes." The word slipped out against her better judgement.

He didn't respond for a long moment, and silence slipped over them. The mule let out a sigh, relaxing into his fate.

"I suppose we could eat Domino, if you're that hungry."

She couldn't hold in a gasp as his words registered. "*Non.* I'll never be that hungry."

His chuckle rumbled low in the stillness, pulling a layer of tension off her chest and leaving her a bit lighter. "Domino and I both thank you." He chuckled again, then the sound dropped away. "I wish I'd brought the food with us. If you get too hungry, please tell me. Yes?"

How would telling him help matters?

But then his hand touched her arm again. "Please?"

She nodded. Then realized how silly that was. "Oui."

"Well then." His hand pulled away, and it sounded like he was making himself comfortable beside her. His coat sleeve brushed against hers. "I suppose we have time to get to know each other. Did I ever tell you of my grandfather's pet monkey?"

She couldn't help the chortle that slipped out. "You haven't mentioned it."

~

drien was just finishing his story about the time his cousin snuck a pet swine into a ballroom overflowing with guests—which was several tales past the one about grand-père's monkey. Madame Standish had seemed to relax by his second outlandish anecdote, and she even chuckled during this one.

If only he could remove the sodden blanket of fear and grim determination that weighed her down. She did have cause for the dour baggage, but if only she'd let him carry some of the load. Trust him just a little. They would weather this storm—and the entire winter—much better together.

He allowed the silence to settle again. It would be nice if she'd share a story or two now. Should he ask?

But she made some kind of movement. A stretch? Then a dainty yawn broke the quiet. "Being still so long makes me sleepy."

"Now is a good time to rest. I still hear the wind outside, and you'll be thankful for the added energy when we walk back." She'd be more comfortable if she rested against his shoulder, but offering it would probably make her skittish.

"I suppose so." She yawned again. A sweet sound that pulled at him in a way he'd do best to ignore.

He leaned back against the wall, trying to settle himself better. This would be a good time to pray.

A half hour later, the steady breathing of the woman beside him drifted closer as her head sank to rest on his shoulder. She'd been leaning into him a little more with each passing moment, and he didn't mind. Not at all, if it made her more comfortable.

And sitting here now, with her softness pressed against his side, his heart thudded a rapid staccato in his chest. She smelled of lye and woodsmoke, two aromas he would have never thought he'd appreciate. Yet mixed with her gentle pressure on his shoulder and arm, they sank through him like the sweetest honey. Wild, soothing.

When she awoke, she wouldn't be happy to find herself using him as a pillow. An image of her reaction slipped through his mind, and he bit back a chuckle. She had so much gumption for such a wisp of a woman, it was fun to see her riled.

Another hour later, he'd almost drifted to sleep, too. But a stirring beside him brought him back to awareness. She snuggled deeper into his shoulder, then seemed to settle back into sleep. A minute later, she shifted again, then yawned with that adorable sound.

Her head lifted from his shoulder, and he held his breath. She was quiet for a moment, probably trying to remember why she was sitting in a dark cave.

"Did you sleep well?" He kept his voice soft so he didn't startle her.

The effort didn't help, for she jumped and turned to face him. "What?"

It was too bad he couldn't see her expression in the darkness. "You were asleep for a while. I should check the weather to see if the snow has stopped."

He pushed to his feet, wiggling his ankles to work the aches out of his benumbed legs. When he stepped around the stone to the edge of the cave, the fury of the blizzard didn't seem to have slowed much. "It's still thick out there."

She stepped up behind him, her presence almost stronger than the blizzard outside. "I think we'll be here a while."

With the world of white outside, he could see her face better. Could see the imprint of his coat where her cheek had rested against it. Those dark lashes framing blue eyes. "It's too bad we can't start a fire. Or at least have some way of getting light."

She turned to look at him. "I stepped on sticks near the back of the cave. If we had something to light a fire with."

He stared into those blue eyes, his mind reaching for ideas. His jacket had pockets sewn into the inside. Perhaps there would be something in there that could help.

After unfastening the buttons, he reached into the left pocket. Nothing. He reached into the right pocket. His fingers brushed leather. He pulled it out and held it up to the light.

The leather fell open to reveal a bit of jerked meat. "I forgot about this. I had it in my pocket the day I found your cabin." He held it out to her. "It's still good."

She gave the strip of meat a look that seemed part dubious, part longing. "We should share it."

Not a chance. "I could stand to miss a meal." He patted his coat in the region of his belly. "You eat this. We'll be back to the cabin before nightfall I'm sure."

She finally took the food and bit into it, turning to watch the snow swirl in a solid white wall as she ate.

~

For a day that felt impossible at one time, it hadn't turned out so bad.

Mary trudged through the snow behind Adrien as dusk fell quickly around them. The blizzard had finally blown itself out, leaving only a blanket of snow that rose well above her knees. If it weren't for the man ahead of her plowing through the drifts with his strong legs, she'd be exhausted by now.

They reached the cabin, and he pulled the door open, then stepped aside for her to pass. She didn't complain against the civility. In truth, she was so exhausted and hungry, she hadn't the strength to complain about anything.

She sank to her knees beside the cold embers of the fire and reached for the pot Adrien had been working with that morning. Had it only been that morning when she'd watched him cooking? She'd been in a pleasant stupor until she stepped outside and started worrying about poor Domino.

A stack of corn cakes sat in the pot, and she reached for two of them. Turning to the man who'd plopped down beside the hearth, she offered one to him. He gave her a weary smile and had the food in his mouth almost before she did.

The bite was perfect. Even cold, the cake seemed to melt in her mouth. She swallowed and bit deep into another.

45

"Good, eh?" Adrien's deep voice teased her from a few feet away, threatening to tug a grin from her.

"The best I've had." She finished that one and moved on to the next. Adrien, too, was well into his second.

When she reached for a third, she saw it was one of the last in the pot. "If you'll tell me what food we have, I can cook something more for us. Maybe the rest of that fox?"

He nodded, then rose and moved to his pack.

The rest of the evening passed in a blur as they ate and made plans for the next day.

"I'll take food to Domino first thing, then do some hunting." He sat by the fire, a mug of ginger root tea in his hands. The firelight danced off his dark features, accentuating the rugged appeal that tied her stomach in knots when she watched him.

"I need to check my traps. I'm sure there's something in them by now. Something very frozen."

He nodded. "If you'll show me where they are, I can keep an eye on them."

That statement should irk her. She was perfectly capable of checking the traps herself. But maybe it would be just as well to have an extra set of eyes watching over them. The more game caught in the traps, the less he'd need to use his bullets, too. She nodded. "We need more firewood. I'll gather it first thing while you take food to the mule. Then we'll go trapping."

He responded with his own nod. "Good plan."

It was a good plan. Wasn't it? Was she letting herself get too comfortable around this man? He wouldn't be here much longer. She'd best be careful not to rely on him.

Not any more than she had to.

CHAPTER 7

Oh, God. Be Thou our strength.
~ Adrien's Journal

$\mathcal{T}$he cramping started in the wee hours of the morning. Like a corset tied much too tight. Much too low.

Mary curled into the pain, cradling the baby inside her. What did this mean? The baby. *Oh, God, the baby. Don't take my child.* This life inside she'd struggled so to protect. Where had she gone wrong?

But so many memories wallowed in her mind, she squeezed her eyes shut against them. She couldn't think about that now. Only God could keep her little one safe. *Please, God. Save my baby.*

The cramping tightened again, bringing with it a wave of nausea. She curled tighter into herself. This had to stop. What could she do to stop it?

Maybe water. Gritting her teeth, she turned over and reached for the cup she'd left on the hearth. Her mouth held a bitter taste, but the water helped wash some of it down.

Pulling herself back under the furs, she wrapped her arms around the baby inside her. As the band of pain tightened again, she tried to whisper a prayer. But her lips wouldn't seem to move. Her heart wouldn't let her form words, even in her mind. *Save my baby. Please.* It was all she could think.

And so, with those words echoing in her soul, she finally let a hot tear slip through her defenses. It slid from the corner of her eye and into her hair. Another followed close behind.

What would she do without her baby? The single bit of hope in her life these past months. The one thing she had to live for. *Oh, God. Please don't take my baby.*

The next few hours passed in a blur. She heard when Adrien rose and stoked the fire, but she held herself as still as possible. She couldn't face him. When he pulled down his snowshoes and laced them on, she breathed out a steady breath. He must be worried about the mule to leave before breaking his fast, but she wouldn't call him back.

The cramping had eased to a lighter ache. Part of her tried to summon hope that the baby might be safe still. Yet, the warm liquid she'd started feeling at least an hour ago told her something very different. She was naïve in many ways, but even she knew the sign that something was terribly wrong.

The cramping ache had moved up to her chest, squeezing her heart in a way that came close to unbearable. *Why, God? Why are you taking this away from me, too?*

Her arms ached, as much from the loss of what they would never be able to hold as from anything else.

She had to pull herself together. Get up from this sickbed and carry on with her share of the work. Adrien already thought her weak and in need of coddling. Just now, it would be so easy to give in and let him do it all. But she couldn't.

She forced herself to sit up, then paused as the room wobbled around her. The skin around her eyes felt tight, like a strip of leather left outside at the mercy of the rain and the piercing sun. She reached for her cup to clear the cotton from her mouth. Empty.

Summoning all the energy she had left, she pushed to her feet and looked around. She should make the morning meal before Adrien returned. Then she had to go for more firewood. What they had now would barely be enough to heat the food. But really. Was any of this important enough to require the strength it would take to accomplish?

She wasn't so sure anything was worth the cost.

~

*A*drien had a whistle on his lips and a gnawing in his belly as he approached the cabin door. He pulled the latch-string and eased the door open, listening for sounds of what might be happening inside.

All seemed quiet, which probably meant Madame Standish had gone to gather firewood. He stepped in, then pulled off his gloves and bent to unlace his snowshoes. Domino had been quite thankful for the cracked corn he'd taken. He'd led the mule out of the cave and turned him loose to find fodder, although he doubted the animal would find grass for a while. He'd need to take food and check him at least twice a day. Which meant his cornmeal wouldn't last much longer.

After hanging the frames on the wall-peg, he turned back toward the fire. Hopefully Madame Standish left something he could eat, as his belly hadn't quite recovered from going without for so long the day before.

The pan sat beside the fire, and he stepped forward, then dropped to his haunches to raise the lid. Looked like corn gruel inside. Not very original, but warm and filling.

A motion to his right snagged his attention, and he looked over at Madame Standish's pallet. The furs hadn't been straightened but lay as though she were still under them.

His heartbeat thudded louder in his ears. Surely she wasn't still lying there. Not unless something was very wrong.

Easing to his feet he stepped closer and peered into the mass of furs. Two of the coverings lay just separate enough to reveal pale skin and a pair of eyes—eyes not closed in sleep. Instead, they simply stared forward.

Was she...dead?

"Madame Standish?" Now his pulse pounded in his ears. He reached down to touch what might be a shoulder. "Are you well?"

Those eyes blinked, releasing the coil that had pulled tight in his chest. Not dead. But...what? "Madame Standish?" He gripped the furs and the shoulder under them, then gave it a light push. Maybe she slept with her eyes open.

She moved then, and he straightened, pulling away from her. She turned onto her back, pushing the covers down, and stared up at him, her look more hollow than he'd ever seen them. The eyes of a dead person, except for the faint lines of red that wove through the edges of white. She'd been crying.

He dropped to his haunches, keeping about an arm's length from her. "What's wrong? How can I help?"

A tiny bit of life seemed to seep back into her gaze, but she still stared up at the ceiling.

"What is it, *mon ami?*"

And then she turned to him, her eyes taking on life. Too much life. Despair seemed to drown them, tears blurring the blue so they looked as stormy as an ocean. He reached for her hand, partly to anchor himself, partly to infuse some bit of comfort into her. "Please, tell me."

She blinked, clearing away some of the moisture. She looked to be coming back to herself. She blinked again, then pulled her hand from his and moved like she would sit up.

He inched backward and stood to give her space. When she pulled her lower half from the covers, the tips of stocking-covered feet peeked out from under her skirt. He pulled his eyes away. It was the first time he'd seen her take her shoes off, even at night.

He turned away as she repositioned her skirts. "I see you made gruel. Shall I scoop some for you, or have you already eaten?"

"None for me." Her voice came out small and fragile, drawing him to her. But he ignored the pull. It was always hard to know what to do when a woman cried. Yet, the depth of despair that had filled her gaze for that single moment made him want to wrap her in his arms. Shield her from the pain she obviously endured.

Was she mourning her deceased husband? That would make sense. Maybe later, she'd feel up to talking about it. His mother always wanted to talk things out when he found her crying.

He gulped down a bowl of the gruel quickly, not making eye contact with the woman who still sat on the edge of her pallet. She seemed to be staring at the far wall, obviously deep in her thoughts. Or memories. Or grief.

At last, he set the empty bowl in the bucket of wash water she must have carried in that morning. Then he turned and met her gaze. "Is there anything I can do for your relief?"

She shook her head. "I'm well. I..." But her thought appeared to fade with the words, and her gaze shifted back to the far wall. Back to her memories.

As quietly as he could, he pushed to his feet and stepped across the cabin to the door. "I'm going to gather firewood. I'll return in a half hour or so." Maybe that would give her time to sort through what troubled her.

If not... *God, I'm going to need a lot of direction with this one.*

One thing he knew for sure, whether she was in the midst of a mental breakdown or not, he wanted to be here for this woman. He'd do whatever it took to make her happy and whole again.

~

*E*nough.

She'd never known how easy it would be to lose one's mind. Just now, she could feel herself sliding toward that edge.

But enough.

She was strong. She'd been through more than one loss. She would endure this one, too.

Pushing to her feet, Mary forced herself to scoop a bit of gruel and swallow each bite. She finished it off with a swig of water, then set the remainder where it would cool until the midday meal.

Then she pulled out her buckskins, both tunic and leggings. She tucked herself into the corner to change, ears straining for any sound of Adrien's return. It wasn't even halfway through the time he said he'd be gone, but there was always the chance he'd come back early.

By the time she did hear his feet crunch in the snow, she'd refreshed herself with a cloth and water, then tidied her sleeping area and the rest of the cabin.

She was washing her dress in the only piggin she had when he stepped inside. He stopped short when he saw her there, on her knees in front of the fire.

Then he approached, his tread soft. "I thought for a moment Indians had come and taken you away, leaving one of their own in your place."

He was probably trying to make her feel better with a bit of levity, but she couldn't summon a smile just now. She did need to say something, though.

Looking up at him, she locked her gaze on his. "I'm sorry for earlier, but I'm fine now. I'm ready to check the traps when you are."

His face sobered, matching her own expression. "I can go hunting with my rifle today. Tomorrow we'll check the traps."

She shook her head. "*Today*, we'll check the traps."

He let out a loud sigh and nodded as he turned to lay his gloves by the door. "Today. Give me a few minutes to warm myself, then we'll set out."

~

The weather was better than Adrien expected as they both trudged out on snowshoes. No sun peeked through the grayish cloud covering, but the wind didn't buffet them either.

With a knife and a hatchet tucked in the belt that wrapped around her buckskin tunic and a satchel slung over her shoulder, Madame Standish looked just like a wilderness voyageur. A rather comely one, at that. He'd not seen her without her heavy fur coat until he stepped into the cabin earlier. That was a sight that wouldn't be leaving his mind any time soon.

Now, she did have her coat tucked around her and a look of steel determination marking her face. No sign of her grief from before. It was almost as if he'd seen a different woman hours ago. A woman so broken that her mind and heart and body had fought to come to terms with her loss. A woman fragile.

Not this mountain warrior who trekked beside him.

She led him around the lake that stretched across one end of the valley. Snow covered the ice so it was almost hard to tell where the land ended and the water began.

A cluster of branches sat at the edge of the bank, and Madame Standish approached them. She stepped out onto the snow-covered ice with only a slight hesitation.

He almost reached to grab her, but he stilled the urge. She must know what she was doing. He did keep his hand ready, though.

She stepped out a few strides to a pole that rose up from the ice. She grabbed it and wiggled, but the base appeared secure in the frozen mass beneath. Dropping to her knees, she pushed the snow away from the pole, then pulled out the hatchet and started hacking at the ice surrounding the wood.

Enough watching. He stepped onto the snow-covered lake, easing his weight into that first step. The ice held without a problem, so he moved forward until he reached her. "Let me do that."

She didn't cease her pounding but seemed to hit harder, whacking at the ice with an intense attack. Her face pinched in a tight grimace, her lips pressed flat and her nose flared. As though the ice were the source of all her pain.

"Madame Standish." He dropped to his haunches behind her, out of swinging range of that hatchet.

She didn't cease her effort until the blade broke through some of the ice, catching on the slush underneath. She heaved the tool upward, grunting like a lumberjack at work. Her effort released the stuck blade and jerked her arm back with painful force.

"Please let me help." He reached out to touch her shoulder.

Still, she didn't acknowledge his presence, just went back to hacking at a new section of ice. Maybe she couldn't feel his touch through her coat and the tension that rose off her like steam from boiling water.

Her blows grew almost frantic now, strike after strike. Her breathing fogged the air, turning to a wheeze that couldn't be healthy. He had to stop her before she injured herself.

"Madame Standish." He squeezed her shoulder enough for her to feel the touch, but not hurt.

No response.

"Mary."

Her blade struck the ice at an angle, sliding to the side and nicking the pole. She made a sound that was half-grunt-half-cry, then doubled over, her hands pulled tight to her middle.

CHAPTER 8

I wish this ache inside would sever my heart the way it has severed
everything else.
~ Mary

*A*drien's pulse hammered as Mary crumpled onto the snow.
Had the blade struck her? He scooted forward and placed a
hand on each of her shoulders. "Are you hurt? What's wrong?"

She curled tighter, pulling herself into a ball. Another cry rent
from her, this time pure anguish. Her shoulders shook under his
hands.

His heart ached as if she were clutching it in balled fists. What
could he do to help? How could he ease her pain?

He'd never had a sister, never been around women much. Only
Mère and Grand-mère. Mère would sometimes grow emotional,
especially after Père had been killed in the military uprising. Grand-
mère would always rub her back and sometimes stroke her fingers
through his mother's thick, honey-blond hair. One woman would
know best how to help another woman, right?

He slid one hand from her shoulder down the fur of her coat, pressing his palm into her back and moving in even circles. Her shoulders shook with her tears, but he kept his movements steady and sure. Doing his best to feed his concern through his touch. She wasn't alone in this. He would do whatever he could to help. If only he could lighten her turmoil.

After long minutes, her sobs subsided. She swiped at her face but stayed bent over so he couldn't see her face. Mère always tried to hide her face, too, when she'd been crying.

He should say something to break the silence. Something to let her know he cared. That she could confide in him, if it helped. He wasn't always good with words, but he could listen. And pray. But he was doing that already.

He cleared his throat and tried to keep his voice gentle. "I'm sorry about your loss. How long has it been?"

She raised her head and turned to look at him. Her eyes were circled in red, and her nose bright against the delicate white of her skin. She seemed to study him. Trying to understand something. "How long?"

"Your husband. I thought he died, but maybe I thought wrong?" Perhaps the man had abandoned her. Still, talking about the loss— however it happened—could help.

She looked away from him, across the snow-covered lake. To the distant mountains. "He did die. Three months ago. But I mourn for my baby." Her voice caught on those last two words.

His breath stilled. A baby? She'd given birth to a baby in these mountains? Perhaps he shouldn't ask, but every part of him craved to know. To understand more of this woman. "How did...the child die?"

She looked at him again, her eyes filling. "She wasn't born yet. I learned of the loss this morning." Her eyes dipped and she looked away, almost as though ashamed.

Her words didn't quite make sense until he mulled them over. *Wasn't born yet?* Then her meaning slammed into him like a punch to his lungs. "Oh, Mary." The words slipped out with a breath as his mind spun.

He knew nothing about such things and didn't want to know the specifics at all. Especially not alone with her in this wilderness. But then his mind replayed the image from a moment ago, her lovely blue eyes, red-rimmed and clouded with tears. She was mourning deeply for this child. Her babe, whom she'd been eagerly awaiting, had died.

This very day.

And here she was, hacking through the ice to check a beaver trap. He couldn't let her do this.

She still faced away from him, so he gripped her upper arms. "I'm so sorry, Mary. I can't imagine what it's like to lose a baby. Your child. What can I do to help?"

She stared toward the mountains again. "There's nothing that can be done." Her voice sounded so fragile, like a blade of grass in a windstorm. As if she might blow away any moment.

His chest ached. He had to do something. "Then let me grieve with you."

Her body went very still under his hands. What had he done? The last thing he wanted was to make her uncomfortable. He just wanted to *help*, but he might have made things worse for her.

Slowly, she turned back to him, and his hands fell away from her arms. Her eyes had that same fragile, shattered look. The look that split him in two.

He couldn't be certain whether he reached for her first, or if she leaned into him, but the distance between them fell away. He pulled her against his chest, tucking her head under his chin, cradling her slender body.

She trembled. Maybe from cold, or maybe not. Then her shoulders shook as before. No sobs slipped from her mouth, but as she curled tighter into his arms, he could feel her tears. Her pain echoed through him.

Lord God, help her. It was all he could do. It had to be enough.

~

*M*ary let herself stay cradled in Adrien's arms until the tears subsided. She shouldn't have, but she couldn't bring herself to resist the comfort of his contact. She'd forgotten how good it felt just to be touched. This one time would be all right.

When she finally pulled her fractured nerves to a semblance of calm, he gave her one of those gentle half-smiles that she'd come to appreciate. He didn't ask for words and didn't press as she pulled back. Just reached for the hatchet and finished digging around the bait pole while she straightened her appearance.

After a few moments of work, he started in on another story about his cousin's pet sow. It was hard to decide whether his tales were purely fictional or if his family simply preferred unusual pets.

But the topic gave her a chance to feel normal again. To lose herself in something trivial.

When they'd pulled up the bait pole, a beaver lay in one of the snare loops. Adrien lifted out the frozen animal with a grim expression, but at least he didn't leave the job to her. Handling the animals was the part she hated. In truth, she wouldn't do it if she had any other way to eat through the winter.

As she reset the snare, he watched her work with an intense expression on his face, asking questions here and there. His queries were intelligent, too. He could probably handle this trap on his own next time.

When they had everything set to rights, he motioned her ahead of him as they stepped off the snow-covered lake. "Would you like to head back now?"

His voice had such a gentle air to it, she turned to look at him. She wasn't used to such kindness. Thomas had been matter-of-fact, using only the words necessary to get the job done. He'd not been mean, just focused on his work. He'd not looked at her like she was a pesky woman, though. Not ever. So she'd concentrated on learning his work so he would notice her. Her efforts had paid off. He'd treated her as an equal in every way.

Adrien didn't treat her like a pesky female either. But the deference he offered, and the way he seemed to think about what she might want, was not something she was accustomed to. It caught her off guard every time.

Now she looked into those dark eyes. They creased at the corners, maybe from the squint caused by daylight on snow. But that gentleness in his gaze couldn't be from the weather. And just now, her heart sank into that look. Let it wrap around her. Strengthen her.

"No, I'm better now. We should check the others while the weather is good."

He studied her as if taking her measure. Then those creases at the corners of his eyes deepened. "All right then."

The next beaver trap they checked didn't take nearly as long but didn't yield a catch either. One of the snares hung loose, but she refastened it without trouble.

"Has there been much game this winter?" He picked up their single catch thus far and followed her toward the snare she'd placed along a rabbit trail.

She let out a snort. Not very lady-like, but certainly better at getting the point across. "The animals were smarter than I, foreseeing this winter that's been colder than any I could imagine. Most of them moved south months ago."

He didn't answer, and something about his silence tensed her shoulders. She glanced over at him. His brow puckered as he walked, his gaze lowered to the ground.

Normally, she would leave a man to his own thoughts. Thomas had always preferred it that way. But something urged her to prompt him. "Your thoughts seem to weigh heavy."

He caught her gaze and offered a half-smile. It didn't reach his eyes, though. "I am just thinking how hard it's been for you. Even with all your experience in these mountains. I'm not sure anyone could have survived this winter on their own. Did you have provisions when the cold started?"

She fought the burn on her face. Fought it hard. She should be angry, not embarrassed. She didn't want this man's pity. Yet, just now, she didn't seem to have the strength to withstand his concern.

So she held her tongue. A minute farther, they reached the cluster of frozen underbrush where one of her snares was set. She toed away the snow that formed a lump over where she'd set the trap. "Looks like this one caught before the first blizzard struck."

Adrien waved her aside and bent to loosen the frozen snowshoe hare. "At least the cold kept the meat from spoiling."

She stepped back out of his way, her snowshoes crunching over the icy snow. In the stillness of the frozen day, the sounds echoed across the white. Or…maybe not an echo.

The faint crackle of something breaking the snow strained at her senses. What *was* that? The fine hairs on the back of her neck rose, and she reached forward to touch Adrien's shoulder.

He looked up, and she motioned for him to be still, then held a silencing finger to her lips.

Without the sounds of his movement, the steady *crunch, crunch* came more clearly. She scanned the snow- and ice-covered brush and brambles. Maybe a bird hopped through the thicket.

But there wasn't any movement in the brush. A large boulder sat next to a handful of trees, and something shifted behind one of the trees.

Her pulse beat faster in her throat. A person? The flicker she'd seen had been too high up to be anything small. Or maybe a chipmunk climbing the tree.

She tried to keep her breathing even. Maybe her heart would take the hint and slow its beating.

Adrien rose to his feet beside her, soundless as an Indian. Had he seen it, too?

That spot beside the tree shifted again. Separated into a furry ear, then an animal's face.

A mountain lion? She reached for Adrien's arm. Something about the creature's ear snagged her focus. That pointed black spike that showed clearly against the white backdrop of the snow. Could it be? The animal stayed rooted with half its face exposed, the other half still hidden behind the tree.

"What is it?" Adrien's words came in a quiet breath.

"I think it's a..." She struggled to think of how to say lynx in French, then settled for the English version. "...a lynx." She switched back to French. "I know of them but have never seen one."

"Is it dangerous?"

She'd heard them compared to a mountain lion, so maybe. Except...they only ate snowshoe hare, didn't they? Which meant...

Her gaze tracked down to the white tuft of frozen fur Adrien had been extracting from the snare. "I think he smells the hare. That's what they eat."

"Should we back away and let him have it?"

Probably. The animal seemed to be wary of them. Maybe just waiting for the right moment to attack? She turned back to the lynx and studied the beady eye staring out of a thick coat of fur. "That might be a good idea. Slowly, so we don't startle him into attacking."

Adrien dipped down to grab his tools and the string holding the beaver, then reached out for her. She took his hand, and they backed away from the snared hare. About thirty paces back, Adrien paused, keeping his voice low. "You think he'll come for it if we stand here?"

She glanced up at him, meeting the sparkle in his gaze. "It would be fun to see, wouldn't it?"

They waited, as still as trees. And while her eyes stayed focused on the cluster of brush and trunks where the lynx would come out, her mind kept drifting down to her hand, still tucked in Adrien's. They both wore gloves, so she couldn't feel his touch or the warmth of his skin. But the fact that he hadn't let go... Did he mean something by it?

Probably just comfort. He was considerate like that. Something she was still getting accustomed to.

As they watched, a shadow moved among the trees, then stepped out toward the uncovered hare. Such an unusual creature, it took a few seconds for her eyes to make out the detail. The animal was about the height of her knee and took the shape of a large cat, except for its black bobbed tail. Its coloring was mottled gray with most of its fur tipped white at the ends, and thick as she would expect during a winter as cold as this one. But the hair looked bushier around the animal's neck, as if it wore a fur scarf.

It moved with a hesitant stride, its wide paws breaking through the thick snow with each step. The long black tips of its ears swiveled as if it heard them. Or smelled them. But it crept forward until it was within a stride of the sprung snare.

Then it leaped onto the carcass, grabbing it like a wolf attacking prey. The dark head shook, then raised up to a regal stance, its conquest hanging from its jaws. Turning, the lynx trotted back toward the trees. Back to safety where it could quell its hunger in peace.

"*Magnifique*." Adrien's low tenor rumbled in her ear.

She turned to look at him. "It was. I've seen animals hunting, but nothing so noble. So...unusual."

His gaze was wide with wonder and seemed to stroke her face, drinking her in. "So many wonders I have discovered in this land. Things I never expected." His voice had grown thick, heavy with meaning.

A meaning she knew in the center of her chest. In her soul. How could he think she herself was a wonder? Something more than a pitiful woman in need of care? A day before, she would have done most anything for him not to look at her with pity. But if it meant the desire she could see deep in his gaze, she wasn't sure the flutter in her middle could withstand it properly.

She swallowed, not quite able to look away. But she must say something. "I..."

Adrien's face softened into his easy smile, his eyes crinkling at the edges. He squeezed her hand—had he still been holding it? "What say we head to the next trap? Maybe we'll get to keep what we find there."

Just like that, he'd made it all better. Taken away the angst in her chest and made her glad he was there.

But Adrien Lockman wouldn't always be there. And then she'd be forced to stand on her own, once again.

CHAPTER 9

My heart and body war within me.
~ Adrien's Journal

*A*drien heaved against the log wall with his shoulder, working the brace into place as he held the logs back. Every muscle in his body strained against the load. Finally, the prop locked to secure the wall.

He eased away from the logs, not quite daring to breathe as he waited to make sure the whole structure didn't come down on him like the walls of Jericho.

It didn't move. *Thank you, Lord.*

Finally, he let himself take in a deep drag of air. He stepped back and studied the little cabin. It stood up straight now, although with logs of so many different thicknesses, it still looked a bit off-kilter. If he could get enough of the cracks chinked, they'd stay much warmer inside. Normal chinking materials wouldn't work just now, as no mudding would dry before it froze.

Maybe stretching furs over the walls on the inside would do for the winter.

He turned and strode toward the door. Mary had gone to feed Domino, but when she returned, he'd ask if she had skins to spare. Until then, it was high time he hang that curtain he'd planned, to give her a little privacy.

He finally worked out a way to hang his rope by the time the crunch of snowshoes sounded outside the cabin. He stood on the hearth, stretching as far up as he could reach to work the cord through an especially wide gap between two logs. There was enough space that he could wrap the rope completely around the log and tie it off.

It would take two people to accomplish, though. One to hold the rope in place inside, and another to feed it over the top of the log on the outside. The inside person would then tie it off.

The door opened and Mary stepped in, only her blue eyes and red cheeks showing between her scarf and hood. Her gaze swept to him as she entered the room, and her eyes widened. She pulled the scarf down to uncover her mouth. "What are you doing?"

He probably looked like he was climbing the wall, stretching up on his toes to keep the cord in place. "Can you hold this in place while I go outside and feed it through the opening above?" She likely wouldn't be tall enough to reach the rope outside, so he'd need to do that part.

She shuffled forward, removing her gloves as she walked. "All right. As soon as I take these snowshoes off."

She removed the frames in quicker time than he ever could, then slipped off her scarf and coat before stepping up behind him. "What do I do?"

"Hold this rope so I can reach it on the outside." He shifted over so she could take his spot.

She moved in close—very close—to reach the rope. He held his breath, but it didn't keep away the heady sense of her nearness. The touch of the wild that clung to her.

Her fingers brushed his hand as she took the cord. "I have it." Her murmur sent a caress of warmth against his cheek.

He stepped off the hearth, more to still the rush of reaction roiling inside him than anything. And when he made it outside, the blast of icy air was just what he needed to cool his inner turmoil.

Good thing he hadn't waited to hang this partition. A little separation from that woman might keep him from something he would regret. Did she feel the same way? How could she, still grieving the loss of her husband and babe?

Yet there were moments that he sensed something within her. A softening. Maybe even attraction.

But he couldn't push her. If she wanted anything more than someone to help endure the winter, she'd have to take the next step. But who was he fooling? She'd made it clear, she didn't even want that much.

Around the side of the cabin, he could see the rope protruding between the logs. Thankfully, the snow had drifted high against the wall, lifting him up enough that he could feed the cord back through the higher crack.

He worked a length of rope through, then called through the wall. "Can you reach the end now?"

"I have it." Not even the logs between them could muffle the clear determination in her voice. Mary Standish wouldn't be deterred once she set her mind to something.

He tromped back to the door, then stepped in.

Mary still stood on the hearth, but didn't have to stretch nearly as far up, for she'd altered the set-up a bit. She'd turned the iron pot upside down on the hearth and now stood on it. Not a sturdy base when she stretched upward at an angle.

He strode forward, hands extended to catch her should the entire arrangement topple. "I can take it now."

"I'm assuming you want this tied." She started to knot the rope around the log.

"Yes, but I can do it. That pot will slide out from under you." He touched her back to steady her.

Just in time, apparently, because her platform slid a bit, and she jerked.

He planted a foot beside the pot to keep it from moving farther and shifted his hands to grip her sides. "Really, Mary. I'll do it. Just get down." If she was hurt in this little project, he'd never forgive himself.

"There. All done." She shifted again as she released the rope.

He had no idea if she could tie a knot that would hold, but he could fix that later, if necessary.

She turned and placed a hand on his shoulder while she peered down to place her feet. No sense in that though. He lifted her the same way he helped his mother down from a carriage.

Except she was nothing like his mother.

Mary gripped both of his shoulders, her blue eyes widening and her mouth forming a soft O as he lowered her. Such a beauty, this woman. Her heart-shaped face with its features perfectly proportioned. Those lips, slightly chapped by the wind. They suited her perfectly. A little roughed-up by the elements, but soft on the inside. And very much in need of kissing.

A stillness settled in the room, pulling his gaze up to her eyes.

They locked on his, a little wildness in them, as though she could read his thoughts. He shouldn't have even been thinking about kissing her. Not after he'd just told himself outside he needed to give her time.

He swallowed, working to gather some moisture in his mouth to apologize. The last thing he wanted was to frighten her.

But then her gaze dipped to his mouth, throwing another log on the blaze he'd been trying to quiet within him. Fire and ice. He wanted more than anything to lower his mouth to hers. But he couldn't. She had to take the first step.

As if she could read his mind, she reached up and raised her mouth to his.

Sweet honeysuckle and pepper. He'd been wrong about her kiss. She was softness, yes, but with fire infused in her touch. A fire that fed the flame inside him.

He forced himself to gentle his touch. Not to lose himself or give in to the inferno inside him. She was so exquisite. A lily to be treasured and cared for.

∽

She'd lost her mind. But she couldn't bring herself to be sorry about it.

Not yet, anyway. Mary gripped Adrien's shoulders, more to hold herself up on quivering legs than for any other reason. She eased away, ending the kiss before she lost the rest of herself.

She'd never had a kiss quite like that. Never. It left her mind and her stomach spinning so that she was breathless.

He reached up to cup her neck, stopping her retreat. Those eyes. Dark and glimmering with the smile that always seemed so near. What did he see in hers? Stark terror?

She shouldn't have kissed him. It gave so many signals that she hadn't meant at all. Couldn't mean. But the way he'd been looking at her. He'd been so near. So gentle. And all his other kindnesses seemed to pile up in her mind. He'd wedged himself so deeply in her heart, in that moment with him so close, her thoughts had turned reckless.

"*Mon lys.*" His thumb stroked her jaw, leaving a warm tingle everywhere it touched.

Had he just called her his lily? She'd never *ever* been called anything so delicate. Yet the way he spoke, the way his eyes drank her in, she could almost believe he saw her that way.

Or maybe she just wanted to believe it. Perhaps she'd let herself be fooled by a handsome face and a gentle touch.

She pulled away, lowering her gaze. She should make some excuse, say something. But the words wouldn't come. Nothing came except the ache in her chest.

So she stepped down from the hearth, snagged her coat from the pile where she'd left it, and then headed out the door.

∽

$\mathcal{H}$e'd pushed her too far.

He knew she wasn't ready for anything more than a helping hand around the place, but he pushed anyway. Even though she started the kiss, he'd jumped in and taken off running. And now, that stiff façade she'd shouldered just before striding out the door made it clear she was through with him. He'd be lucky if she let him stay the night. Perhaps he should go share the cave with Domino.

For now, he might as well complete the job he'd started. It wasn't hard to finish hanging the cord, and he used a couple of the furs from Mary's pallet to form a curtain. Hopefully she'd not be irritated that her bed was a little lower if it gave her some privacy.

Next, he scanned the room for something to chink the walls with. There really wasn't anything, except maybe furs. And he'd have to ask Mary before touching any more of those.

Speaking of Mary, where had she gone? Escaping from him, surely. But she shouldn't have to stay out in the cold just to keep away from him. Maybe if he went out to gather firewood, she'd come back to the cabin. Of course, maybe she wouldn't know he'd left, and they'd both be out in the cold, avoiding each other. But he'd have to take that chance.

Besides, they always needed more firewood.

He strapped on his snowshoes and grabbed his hatchet, then headed toward the little cluster of trees where they'd seen the lynx a few days before. He could check the snare while he was there.

By the time dusk began to coat the landscape in shadows, he'd cut a sizeable stack of wood. He'd best start hauling it back to the cabin now if he was to finish before dark fell in earnest.

With his arms loaded down, he paused at the door to the cabin. The latch string was out, which either meant Mary hadn't returned, or she'd not locked him out just yet. He made a racket as he raised the latch, to give her warning if she was inside.

As his gaze scanned the room, it snagged on Mary's lithe form, kneeling by the fire. She didn't turn to face him when he dumped the load where they normally stacked the firewood. The branches already there proved she'd been of the same mind. At least they'd have plenty of fuel for the fire.

"I have a few more loads to bring in. And there was another hare in the snare. Would you like the meat for tonight?" He tried to keep his voice genial, as though this evening were no different from any other. Maybe if he pretended that kiss had never happened, she wouldn't mount her defenses as high as they had been before.

"The evening meal is almost ready. We can eat the hare tomorrow." Her voice was quiet. Not the stiff distance he expected, just...quiet.

Should he offer an apology? Maybe this wasn't the best time. "All right. I'll be back in a few minutes."

She didn't turn to him as he strode toward the door, but the brisk efficiency in her movements and the line of her shoulders showed her determination. Exactly what he'd been expecting. She had more strength of will than a cart horse headed home. But he couldn't complain about that part of her character when it was one of the things he loved best about her.

One of the many things.

Along with her beauty and ingenuity and intelligence. The one thing he'd not been able to ascertain was her faith. Did she know the Father? She'd not shown resistance the times he'd mentioned trusting God or when he'd prayed before eating, but she'd not spoken of God either.

Lord, show me how to help her. Because the matter of her faith was the only thing that kept him from losing the rest of his heart to her. She'd need time, for sure, to heal from the loss of her husband and babe. And he'd wait as long as she needed for her heart to be ready.

Is she Your plan for me, Father? Make my way clear.

CHAPTER 10

Where are my tethers? Something to hold me firm? I feel cast about with each
new adversity.

~ Mary

"The sky looks dark. I think we'll see snow again before the day is through." Mary pulled off her gloves the next morning after gathering fresh snow to wash the dishes from the morning meal. "I moved Domino yesterday to a place where he could dig for fodder, since the corn is getting low."

Adrien looked at her from where he stood in the middle of the floor, hands propped at his waist. "That was wise. I'll check him later this morning."

She shook her head, maybe more quickly than she should. "I'll do it. I know exactly where he is." And she couldn't stay cooped in this cabin with her thoughts all day. She needed to keep moving.

He studied her, his gaze thick enough it was like he could read her thoughts. "All right." He turned back to focus on the wall, as he'd been doing when she entered. "I'd like to chink some of these openings between the logs. I braced up that wall yesterday so it doesn't slant"—he pointed to the right side—"but that made some gaps wider. I don't think chinking mud will work until the weather warms, but we could spread furs over the wider openings." He turned to her. "What do you think?"

They wouldn't be able to cure the furs from this winter until spring, but she still had a decent stack she'd been sleeping on. She moved toward her bed, which now sat hidden behind the curtain Adrien had hung. A thoughtful touch. "How many do you need?"

"It depends on how big they are. Maybe three or four."

She pulled five from the stack. It lowered the height of her bed considerably, but she'd do fine without them. Then she ducked back around the curtain and handed them over. "As soon as I clean the dishes, I'll help hang them. Then I'll check the mule."

He dropped his focus to the furs in his hands. "That's all right. Go check Domino. I can do this alone."

Heat crept up her neck as she turned away, too. The last time they'd attempted a project together, the closeness had affected her much more than it should have. It was probably best they go their separate ways today. If he needed help when she returned, well...she'd do what she had to.

Adrien was already mounting one of the furs when she strapped on her snowshoes and slipped outside. She headed toward the cave first, the easiest route around to where she'd left Domino, although it would take a few minutes longer. A half hour later, she reached the small flat area that had been a grassland before winter struck. She and Domino had dug out a section of stringy brown fodder when she'd left him there with loose hobbles the night before. The areas he'd pawed through the snow were apparent as she made her way through the clearing.

But no wooly-coated mule.

She tracked his progress across the field and found the spot where he'd wandered through the woods. The closeness of the trees pressed down on her as she tromped through their dim shelter. A howl sounded in the distance, sending a shimmer down her spine. She'd not heard wolves in weeks, but their cry always tightened a knot in her stomach. They'd never bothered her and Thomas, so she had no reason to worry.

Except... She'd never had a mule around either. Would the wolves be hungry enough to attack Domino?

Maybe, with game so scarce this season. Perhaps she should take him back to the cave. Or maybe he would be safest in the cabin. She didn't relish the thought of mule droppings on the dirt floor, but they could keep it as clean as possible. Not ideal, but survival trumped cleanliness in the wilderness. Especially in a winter this treacherous.

She'd been traipsing through the woods for a quarter hour at least and still hadn't caught sight of Domino. Soon, she'd reach the spot where they'd seen the lynx. Might that animal be lingering in the area, looking for easy prey? Larger prey? If it were hungry enough, it would surely attack a mule intent on finding grass.

Her hand sought the knife strapped to her belt, resting on the hilt of it. This was the only protection she'd brought with her, but she could use it to its full capacity.

She kept her senses sharp as she stepped out of the trees and scanned the underbrush where her snare was set. A bird hopped through the snow-covered brush, but nothing else moved. The trap hadn't been sprung either. She paused to adjust it, then straightened and looked around one more time.

A sound drifted through the thick air. A wail, almost like the piercing cry of a bull moose.

Or maybe a mule in pain.

She sprinted toward the sound. Or tried to.

On her second step, the tip of her snowshoe snagged in the snow, sending her sprawling.

The cry pierced the air again. Definitely Domino. And something was very wrong.

She pushed up and jerked the tie on each of her snowshoes. She could move faster without them. The snow was up to her knees, but she left the frames behind and bounded through the stuff toward the mule's cry.

Somewhere near the lake. Or at least, that's where it seemed. Hopefully, the faint echo wasn't distorting the sound.

Domino's wild *haw, hee-haw* sounded again, over and over in an urgent scream.

God, let me find him. She could imagine so many reasons the mule might cry out like that. A mountain lion. The lynx. Maybe the wolves had caught his scent and come to make a meal of him.

Her boot snagged in the snow again, and she almost landed on her face once more. But she scrambled and steadied herself. The lake wasn't much farther ahead. Had Domino wandered to the edge? Even if he ventured out on the ice, it should be plenty strong enough to hold him.

As the wide span of frozen water came into view, a dark figure writhed on the white surface, near the pile of sticks that marked the beaver dam. Exactly where her bait pole extended above the ice. Had Domino somehow become caught on the stick? That didn't make sense, as she'd removed the halter rope for precisely that reason—so he wouldn't snag it on anything. Surely he could snap the pole easily if it had caught in his tail.

The mule's cries escalated as she came within thirty strides from him, and she poured more energy into her run. He looked to be down on his front knees, with his hindquarters sticking up. Had he broken a leg?

Oh, God, no. A broken leg would be fatal for the mule. *Not Domino.*

When she neared the edge of the lake, she slowed to a walk, trying to keep her movements easy so she didn't frighten him even more. "Easy, boy. Stay calm."

A splash sounded, drawing her gaze down to where the mule's front legs rested on the ice. Except he wasn't kneeling there.

His legs had broken through.

She sprinted the last few steps and dropped to her knees beside the area where they'd hacked through the ice to check the beaver trap. The ice must have been thin there, and when the mule stepped on the spot, his weight pushed him all the way through. Although what possessed him to walk to the place, she had no idea.

She rubbed a hand down the mule's neck. "Easy, boy." The animal's eyes shone huge, rimmed in white, but he seemed to calm as she stroked him. Then he jerked backward, struggling to pull himself up out of the water.

It was no use. He'd never get his front feet out without something to step on.

She reached for one of his legs but could just grip the top of the upper bone. She tried to work her fingers under the mule's chest, so maybe both of their efforts would give him the strength he needed to pull out of the water.

No matter how she strained, the mule never budged.

Mary leaned back and scanned the animal again. If she had a rope, maybe she could fasten a halter or even wrap a strap around his body to pull him out. That might be the only way they'd save Domino.

She'd not thought to bring a rope with her, so she'd have to run back to the cabin. And Adrien could help. Together, they could get the mule out.

She patted Domino's neck as he struggled again to free himself from the icy hold. His thrashing wasn't so violent anymore, as though he grew weary. How long would he last in this frigid water? Did mules get frostbite? Probably not, but he could certainly freeze to death.

She couldn't let that happen.

Pushing to her feet, she turned and jogged toward the lake's edge. It would take at least ten minutes to run to the cabin, and the same to trek back.

A figure moved in the snow on the bank, drawing her focus. Something gray, but her eyes couldn't seem to focus on the object. Then her vision narrowed on the animal, and her breath stuck.

A wolf.

Her pulse clamored in her throat as she slowed to a halt. Another wolf followed a couple lengths behind the first. Then two more on that one's tail.

The pack must have heard Domino's brays. The cry of an injured animal. The perfect prey for hungry wolves.

She took one charging step toward them, flapping her arms. "Shoo! Get out of here!"

They moved, but not away. Just sideways along the bank, never taking their beady eyes off her. Or rather, off Domino.

Waving her arms again, she took another stomping step toward them. "Go on! Git!"

The lead wolf veered away, then turned and followed its tracks back the way it had come. The others followed its path. Were they leaving? Or just pacing? Circling.

Panic welled in her throat. She couldn't leave Domino alone with the wolves. They'd charge in for the kill the moment she walked away from the trapped mule. And Domino wouldn't last much longer. Though the whites of his eyes still showed wild, he'd almost ceased his struggle against the ice.

She made another short charge toward the wolves, clapping her gloved hands together and yelling at them.

One of the rear wolves turned and snarled at her, baring wide white fangs. A warning, no doubt. She'd be easy prey against four sets of those powerful jaws.

Even though it didn't seem possible he could hear her all the way back at the cabin, she lifted her head and cupped her hands around her mouth. With all the strength she could summon, she screamed, "Adrien!"

~

Adrien had hung all the skins except this last, although a couple of them weren't very secure. He'd have to whittle some pegs to hold them in place better.

But first, this wolf fur needed to be mounted near the top of the wall opposite the fireplace. He couldn't reach the top, even if he stood on the pot. Maybe if he had a stick, he could work the top edge of the hide into the crack between the logs. It should be secure there. Unfortunately, he couldn't find any rods the right shape or size in the cabin, so he'd have to go out and find one. Maybe bring in more firewood while he was at it.

He slipped into his coat and worked the buttons, then grabbed his gloves. It'd be easier to walk in the snowshoes, but they were such a bother to put on. Still, they kept the lower half of his trousers dry, so he bent to lace them over his boots.

Outside, the woolen gray clouds hung low. There wasn't much wind, a blessing to be sure. He headed toward the patch of woods where he'd first built the shelter for Domino, which had collapsed before the second blizzard.

The wind made an eerie sound. Or...not the wind.

He paused, stilling his body to focus his senses. There wasn't enough wind to make that cry. His heart thudded loud in his ears. Could it have been Domino's bray?

Maybe the mule was just greeting Mary, but she'd left a long time before. She should have been with him long before now. Something didn't feel right.

There. The cry came again, a howling noise that sounded vaguely like...his name. His mind came alive, and his body sprang forward.

Mary needed him.

CHAPTER 11

I've done all I can, yet is it enough?
~ Adrien's Journal

"Adrien!" Mary's voice had grown hoarse, but her desperation welled like boiling water in a sealed cauldron.

She glared at the wolves. They'd crept closer, now only a dozen strides away. Two sat eyeing her while the others paced around them. How much closer would they dare come?

"Adrien!"

Her calling wasn't helping. She was too far from the cabin. He wouldn't hear. She had to find another way to save Domino.

Dropping to her knees beside the mule, she stroked his lathered neck. He didn't even try to struggle anymore. She could no longer see the whites of his eyes. He barely lifted his muzzle above the snow as she knelt beside him.

"Stay with me, boy. Don't give up." She peeled off her glove and stroked his sweat-dampened shoulder. He felt cool to the touch, but maybe that was the blast of cold air hitting her own skin, affecting her senses. She scrubbed her fingers in circles on his neck and shoulder. Perhaps this would invigorate his blood and wake up his chilling body.

It could only be a temporary fix, though. She had to find a way to get him out.

While keeping up the rubbing, she eyed the bait pole. If she could work it under his belly, just behind his front legs, maybe she could pry the mule out. She grabbed at the stick, knocking it over with her clumsy left hand.

On the second try, she gripped it, then worked it under the mule's body. Domino had pressed the snow down under him, but she was able to clear enough to wedge the thin pole behind his legs. Would the stick be strong enough?

"Come on, boy. Let's get you out." She eased up on the stick, willing it to make a difference. Any difference.

The crack of splintering wood shattered her desperate hope.

She dropped to her haunches, letting the icy snow pierce her buckskin breeches and tunic. It wasn't going to work. Nothing was going to work.

She crawled back to Domino's head, her hands sinking into the icy snow. *Don't let him die, Lord. Please.*

All her fear and resentment and anguish swept over her like a crashing avalanche, and she burrowed into Domino's coat. "You can't leave me, too." The sobs welled from her deepest core, swelling in her throat as they clogged her breathing, forcing their way out in agonizing gasps. "I can't...do this."

Her body purged itself with sob after aching sob, her heart coughing up every ache that had pressed upon her in these past months. Years even. A lifetime of longing and losing and craving something more.

Someone. Someone to love her exactly as she was. Outspoken. Unfashionable. Determined. More comfortable with animals than people.

Something touched her shoulder, and she jerked back, spinning to face the assailant.

"It's all right." Adrien. His handsome face, those smile lines at the edges of his eyes. Those eyes that now looked at her with such tenderness, it made the tears slip down her face anew. "It's all right." He pulled her close, and though part of her wanted to pull away, she clung to his collar.

"I can't…" She motioned toward Domino as she tried to stop blubbering long enough to speak.

"He's put himself in a fix." Adrien still held her tight, one hand stroking her arm.

She had to stop this. Domino needed their help. *Help me, God.* She took in a tremulous breath, then exhaled it. "I couldn't get him out."

Adrien reached out to stroke the mule's neck, still keeping her tucked into his chest with the other hand. "How can we help you, boy?"

The mule turned to look at him, apparently reenergized by the presence of his friend. Adrien had the same easy way with the mule that he did with her. And she understood exactly why Domino put such trust in him. This man had an inner strength that drew her heart with steady power.

"I couldn't lift him. I was going back to get you and a rope, but then the wolves came." She pushed away from Adrien to look over his shoulder. The circling predators had backed away considerably.

"I tried to run them off, but I'll need a gun to get rid of them completely." He leaned back, letting the cold air slide in where his warmth had been. "I'd better go get that rope and gun. Stay here with our boy."

She nodded, then turned her focus back on the mule. Even now, she was helpless to do anything other than stroke him. This was a good opportunity to stop the tears, but she couldn't seem to make them abate. How did Adrien stay so strong? Maybe his strength was simply because he was a man. Although, Thomas hadn't emanated the steady gentleness that drew her the way Adrien did.

Something inside this man made him different. And whatever it was, she wanted it. To be the same way. To have the inner knowing. The inner calm that inspired others to trust him.

*T*hank God Mary hadn't moved when Adrien made it back to her.

Domino looked rough. They had to get the mule out of the ice if he were to have any chance of survival. *Lord, don't let his legs be broken.*

As much as this boy had been a good friend over the past months, Adrien had been just as worried about Mary when he'd first spotted them before. It wasn't like this strong woman to give way to emotion. But losing so many people could weaken any person, even a woman with nerves of iron and determination to match. *Lord, use this struggle to turn her to You.*

He placed the rifle in her lap. "Can you take care of the wolves while I get the rope tied around Domino?" Giving her a job to do might help her, and he had no doubt Mary Standish could take down a wolf or two, probably better than he could.

She took the rifle and stood without a word, leaving him to the task of figuring out how to get the mule out of the icy water. Perhaps if he fastened the halter first, then if Mary pulled at his head and Adrien worked with his legs, the three of them could do it together.

No, the four of them. They'd never get the mule out without Divine intervention. With a steady prayer on his lips, he set to work fastening the rope.

Domino barely jerked when the rifle shot split the air.

A high-pitched yelp sounded from the direction of the wolves, but Adrien only raised his focus long enough to confirm Mary was safe.

Which she was, and hastily reloading the rifle's breech. The other wolves would likely be gone before the gun was ready, but if she thought she could shoot a second wolf, it was worth a try. They'd need all the meat. And he knew without a doubt she wouldn't waste a shot. Not when bullets and powder were so hard to come by.

She was back by his side in another minute. He spared her a glance as he tied the halter on Domino's head. She looked better. Not quite as raw, more grim.

It only took a moment to relay his plan to her. "Here's the rope."

She took it and moved to the other side of the mule so she'd have a better angle, then gave a tug on his head. "Come on, boy. Wake up. You're going to have to work at this, too."

Adrien positioned himself at the mule's legs. "We'll try this first. If it doesn't work, I'll get a thicker log to use as a wedge. Your idea was a good one."

He motioned toward the fragment of stick poking from under Domino, but she looked away. How much had she gone through before he arrived? More than he wanted to think about.

"On the count of three." With the word, he put all his effort into pulling the mule. That didn't seem to help, so he jumped to Domino's other side and pushed. The animal scrambled, but the ice seemed to have frozen around his legs.

Adrien kicked at the ice, breaking through to free the mule's limbs. Frigid water slushed over his boot, but he ignored the icy tingles that made their way through the leather.

"Pull now!" He ducked behind the mule and braced his feet in the snow, then pushed with every ounce of strength God had given him.

Little by little, Domino inched backward, his legs pulling out of the icy hole. His knees came into view, and Adrien added a little more oomph into his push, although where the strength came from, he couldn't have said.

"He's coming!" The excitement in Mary's voice surged through him, giving him an extra burst of energy.

Then, like a limp weight, Domino's body slid sideways. Out of the hole. Out of the water.

Adrien collapsed onto snow, his face in the slushy indentation where the mule's warm body had melted some of the snow. He was too spent to even pull his face from the sludge.

"Good boy." Mary's voice came in a steady rhythm above him. Hopefully, she was working to warm the mule's legs.

God, don't let them be broken. He should stand up and help her.

"We need to get him up, then back to the cabin."

Her words were the final push he needed to force his weary body to straighten, then push to his feet. His right foot had grown numb where he'd kicked through the ice in the hole. His trousers were wet. Not good in these temperatures.

Mary followed his gaze, and the wrinkle in her brow probably meant she guessed his thoughts. "You both need to get back to the fire."

Together, they pushed Domino to his feet, and the poor boy stood with his head drooping.

Adrien gave him a firm pat on the neck. "Let's see if you can walk." It would truly be a miracle if the animal came out of this with no ill effects.

With some firm nudging, Adrien finally prodded the mule forward. Mary picked up the rifle where she'd laid it on his powder bag and followed them off the ice.

"Can you walk him back while I carry the wolf?" He held the rope toward her.

"Leave the wolf. I'll come back for him later, after you're both settled." She'd regained most of her determined air, yet not all of it. Her voice and gaze still held a bit of vulnerability he hadn't seen often in her.

But he shook his head, and not just to test that hint of vulnerability. "Some other animal will get the meat. I'll bring it now."

She let out a grunt that clearly sounded her exasperation, but she didn't argue again, just took the mule's lead line. She knew he spoke the truth. She'd faced the predators in this land before.

CHAPTER 12

I must know. For once, I long to understand my lack.
~ Mary

When they finally traipsed into the cabin, Adrien's shoulders felt as though they'd worked a full week in the last hour alone. First pushing Domino out of the ice, then dragging the wolf carcass back to the cabin. Although in truth, it was the strain of his fear for Mary that had tightened his muscles the most.

She buzzed around them in the warmth of the cabin, stoking the fire, melting snow into water, preparing a warm, thick corn gruel for him and Domino both.

"I'm not sure what I should think about you feeding me the same thing as my mule, but I suppose I can be naught but thankful." He raised his spoon to Mary as she gave him the makings of a smile. Then she turned back to her work at the fire.

His frozen foot had warmed with only a bit of pain, so hopefully he'd escaped frostbite. And Domino was gulping down his feed with eager lips. Maybe he had escaped the experience unscathed.

Adrien motioned toward the hearth. "Sit, Mary. Rest yourself. You've been through more than me. It's time to rest."

She glanced at the spot where he motioned and started to shake her head, but paused partway through the act. Her face seemed a jumble of emotions that furrowed her brow and pinched her full lips into a thin line. It was hard to read her thoughts through the muddle.

She sat, her hands pressing the stone on either side of her, as though she would jump up any moment. He knew that look. Sometimes, his mother would get a similar edginess when she needed to talk something out. The question now was, would Mary open up to him without prodding?

She reached for her cup of tea, steeped from roots she'd gathered the last few days. He took a sip of his own. Bitter, but at least it had flavor.

After setting her cup down, she looked to be trying to relax. But the line of her shoulders made it clear the effort hadn't been successful.

He cradled his warm cup in both hands. "You didn't say how you found Domino in the ice. Did you search for him long?" Maybe that would get her started.

She looked at him, her eyes rounding as if she were picturing a scene. That blue gaze dragged him in every time he looked at her.

"I went back to the clearing where I left him. It looked like he'd found some fodder through the snow, but he wasn't there. It was easy enough to track him, though. I feared he might have run into that lynx, but when I reached the spot, I heard Domino braying near the lake." She finally blinked for the first time. "I suppose my snowshoes are still there where I first heard him. He sounded so panicked, I just took them off and ran. I'd heard wolves before that and was afraid they'd found him." She drifted into silence, her gaze focused somewhere over his shoulder. Somewhere deep in her memories.

Then she inhaled sharply, blinked again, and looked at him. "Adrien, why does Domino trust you so implicitly?"

He raised his brows. Not the direction he'd expected her to take. "You mean, when we were getting him out of the ice?"

She shook her head. "No. I mean...yes. But not just then." She pressed her mouth shut and seemed to be measuring her words. "I noticed it that first time I tried to move him to the cave. Something about your presence seems to soothe him. You don't get ruffled, and he just does whatever you ask. You have this way about you that...I don't know, just makes people and animals want to trust you. What is it? How did you become like that?"

His spirit stirred in his chest, almost pinching as certainty flooded him. He knew exactly what she was asking, and this was his moment to make all the difference. *Thanks for the chance, Lord, but please, give me the words.*

She studied him with such intensity, as if she were trying to read the answer in the lines on his face.

He met her gaze. "It's not me that inspires trust, it's what shines through me. Or rather...Who."

The pretty skin on her forehead wrinkled as she took in his words. But he'd not given her enough detail to understand yet. "If you see any good in me, anything that inspires trust, it's God's spirit who dwells within me. *He* is the good in my life. My strength. My peace." The words sent a slew of conviction through him, even as they slipped out of his mouth.

Had he turned to God when his spirit felt such unrest after the June uprising in France? He stared at the far wall, allowing the truth to come to him. No, he'd made up his own mind to leave all the bloodshed and set off for the Canadas. *Forgive me for not seeking You, Lord.*

He reached for Mary's gaze again. This part was important. "I don't always take the right actions. In fact, I rarely do. But when I chose to submit my will and my plans and my very heart to God, He became a part of me. The best part. And my God is so good, he wants to do the same for everyone."

Mary's mouth parted, as though she wanted to speak. *Guide this conversation, Lord. Show her Your heart.* She leaned forward. "But if God does it for everyone, why do you seem different? Why don't I feel it, too?"

"Because I've accepted the gift of His presence in me. It's a choice we all have."

She leaned back, the indentions in her brow giving evidence to the thoughts swirling inside. She had much to ponder, no doubt.

He waited a few more minutes to see if she had more questions, but she seemed lost in her thoughts. Finally, he rose and placed his cup on the hearth. "I'll skin the wolf now."

A murmur was her only response, although he couldn't decipher the words.

She's in Your hands now, Lord. But then, that's where she's always been.

◞◟

*M*ary scrubbed at the blanket, then dipped it back in the pot of water. This would be so much easier in a creek, but she didn't have one close by, and she had to do something to keep busy.

When I chose to submit my will and my plans and my very heart to God, He became a part of me. The best part.

She'd been stripped of so much the past months, it felt as though she had no *best part* left. Her whole being was nothing but the dregs of who she'd once dreamed of becoming. What would it be like to submit her will and plans and very heart to a greater Being? Someone who could take what little she had left to give and, maybe...just maybe...make something better from her.

I want that, God. Whatever you can do with me, please...do it. Her chest ached with the intensity of the thought. She was all in. No turning back.

She fell back on her heels, closing her eyes as she sank into the moment. The burden pressing on her chest didn't seem quite as heavy. A warmth caressed her face as she turned it upward. Maybe it was just heat from the nearby fire, but the peace that seemed to seep into her pores came from something very different.

A sound behind her crept through the moment, and she forced

herself to open her eyes and turn. But she couldn't quite pull the smile from her face. Every part of her felt lighter.

Adrien stood just inside the doorway, watching her. His expression held a bit of curiosity, a bit of concern. As he studied her, one side of his mouth tipped, and the corners of his eyes creased.

He shucked his gloves and walked toward her, unbuttoning his coat as he came. "You look less troubled than when I left." He dropped to his knees by the fire, the pot of wash water the only thing separating them.

The relief—nay, joy—welling in her chest made her want to gush her news. But how to tell him. *What* to tell him. She wasn't sure she quite understood what her simple choice had wrought.

So, she dropped her gaze to the blanket and started scrubbing it again. But she couldn't quite conceal the grin stretching her face. "I… decided you were right. This once." She kept her tone light, which wasn't hard to do.

"Right?" His voice held more than a little hope. Cautious hope.

She dared a glance up at him through her lashes. "I made my choice. The same one you made."

He was by her side in an instant. Wrapping her in his arms so quickly, she barely had the chance to drop the wet blanket before he enveloped her. She curled her arms into his chest, breathing in the scent of him. The feel of him. The feeling of being cared for. And now, doubly so. By Adrien. By God.

CHAPTER 13

With the spring comes yearning.
~ Adrien's Journal

TWO MONTHS LATER

*A*drien stood at the corner of the cabin and soaked in the warmth of the March sun, which was doing its best to break through the layers of snow. These past months hadn't been easy, but they may well have been the best of his life. Working side-by-side with Mary to keep them fed and warm through the dark winter days.

From the day she'd given her heart to the Father, the change in her had been gradual, yet marked. She was still competent and determined, but little by little, her strength seemed to come from a different place. A solid foundation. Christ within.

When he offered to read aloud from his Bible in the evenings, she'd listened with furrowed brow. Sometimes asking a question, sometimes commenting on the stories.

And she laughed. Just that morning, she'd chuckled when Domino knocked the bowl from his hands as he tried to feed the mule. Her joy held a clear, vibrant sound. Like her spirit had finally been unfettered.

The cabin door opened behind him, and he turned to watch that very woman step outside. Every time she came near him, his heart leapt in his chest. His pulse thumped harder. And he couldn't wipe a silly grin from his face.

He reached for her hand as she approached. She took it but gave him a curious glance. He'd not kept his attraction a secret, but he'd done his best to keep his hands to himself for the most part. She was too much temptation to allow himself even one more kiss while they lived in such close quarters.

But soon. Lord willing.

He pulled her closer and slipped his arm around her waist.

She leaned her head against his shoulder. "I thought you were going to gather wood."

He smiled into her hair. "I stopped to enjoy the sun. We haven't seen much of it lately. Do you think it might be here to stay?"

She let out a long breath that could be a sigh. "Maybe not yet. But it's nice while it lasts."

His gaze wandered to the narrow trail where the mountains formed a V. "I wonder when the snow will melt in the big valley through that pass?"

Her body stiffened beside him. Then she straightened, pulling away. He tried to tug her back, but she turned to face him. "Are you anxious to leave?" Her face held what she probably meant as lack of concern, but he could make out the edges of vulnerability.

His hands itched to pull her close again. Maybe shuck his gloves and stroke her cheek, then kiss her until he'd banished every thought of him leaving from her mind.

But he held himself still and willed her to see the truth in his eyes. "I'm not leaving you, Mary."

She wrapped her arms around herself, that vulnerability sneaking out a bit more. "I know you need to. You have plans."

He did step forward this time, but he only slipped his hand around one of her arms. "Yes, I do have plans."

It must have been the teasing tone of his voice that made her blue eyes widen. And when her lips parted—probably in shock—he just couldn't stop himself.

~

*M*ary gripped Adrien's arms to keep herself upright. She'd had only a flash of warning before he pulled her close and lowered his mouth to hers. Her lips hadn't been ready. Her mind struggled to catch up.

Then the warm taste of him broke through her fog, and she inhaled, coming alive. This was Adrien, kissing her with a thoroughness that infused her senses. And oh, heavens, did she respond.

These past months of living and working so near him had been a strain. A wonderful torture. And for just this moment, she broke free of it. Responding to his kiss with the love that had filled her more each day. Each hour. Growing so that the thought of him leaving had plunged a knife of desperation into her.

But if he was leaving...

She forced herself to regain control, to pull back. If this was his way of saying good-bye, well...

They were both breathing hard, the air fogging between them as she tried to step away. But his hands held her waist, not giving a bit.

"Adrien, I—"

"Mary." He tugged her closer, and she let him. Reluctantly. It was almost impossible to resist the pull of this man.

She inhaled his presence as he lowered his forehead to rest on hers.

"Mary." The rich timbre of his voice drew her like a bee to nectar. She could feed on it for days.

"Yes?" Her voice sounded too breathy in her ears, but she didn't try for a better tone.

"When I go settle in that wide valley, I don't want to go alone. I'd like you to be there with me. To build a life with me, working together. As my wife."

She sucked in a breath with that last word, his meaning crystalizing in her mind. Her mind, her heart, did she dare hope?

He lifted his head a little, and she could feel his gaze studying her, although she kept her focus on his jaw. His mouth.

He lifted her chin with his finger so she had to meet his gaze. Those beautiful brown eyes. The faint creases that usually lined the corners had mostly smoothed with the concern tenting his brow.

He was so good, this man. How could she ever deserve him? She wasn't quite the broken, half-starved woman he'd found almost three months ago, but she still had so much to learn. About God's love. His goodness. Emotion clogged her throat, raising the burn of tears to her eyes. The same love and goodness shone from Adrien's eyes now.

Except there was also a fair amount of worry glimmering in his gaze. "What is it, love? What's wrong?" He moved his gloved hand to cup her cheek, then thumbed away the tear that broke through her defenses. "You don't have to answer now. Take time to decide. Seek God's guidance." Those sweet, gentle eyes seemed to wrap around her in a warm embrace.

She worked to swallow down the lump clogging her throat. "I don't need time. I would love to be your wife, Adrian Lockman. But… are you sure? You're not asking me just because I'm the only woman within two week's ride?"

She held her breath but worked to force a smile to lighten the question.

His gaze stroked her as his mouth found the smile she'd been trying for. "I've never been so sure of anything in my life." And then he kissed her again. A seal. A promise of much to come.

91

EPILOGUE

One Month Later

"Do you think we'll find a priest at this fort?" Mary focused on the back of Adrien's shoulders as she walked, the same strong shoulders she'd been following for over a week now.

He turned to look at her, those smile lines she loved creasing the corners of his eyes. He slowed to let her catch up, then slipped an arm around her waist as they continued walking together. Her, him, and the mule—side by side. "If we don't, I'm sure there will be someone authorized to perform weddings. Or...we could always choose to say our vows only before God?"

She ignored the gaze he cut toward her. He knew her opinion on the matter. Still, she couldn't help responding. "When a deed is important, it's worth the effort to do it right."

His warm chuckle drifted on the breeze. "That's my Mary. Once she makes up her mind, none dare withstand her."

The teasing in his tone tugged at the corners of her mouth. "If there's none at the fort who can marry us, I suppose we can discuss other options."

That chuckle again. But the way his hand pulled her closer fed a warmth that bloomed in her chest and spread throughout her. She'd never thought it possible to feel so loved.

~

*T*wo days later, they finally reached a cluster of rough buildings that looked more civilized than anything she'd seen in almost a year. A few men milled among them, bearded and clothed in buckskins and furs. Thomas would have fit in well here.

Her heart didn't pang as much at the memories anymore. They were a part of her life. *He'd* been a part of her life, but she was moving into a new stage now. With hope for the future. Something she hadn't been sure she'd ever have again. There was a freedom in that. A freedom she'd been craving longer than she'd realized.

One of the men strode from the shelter of the buildings while the others hung back, watching. Adrien spoke to him in French, and the man responded in kind with a welcome.

Praise be. Not only were they friendly, there was at least one Frenchman in the group, so she wouldn't need to translate.

They followed the man toward the others, and Mary almost asked the question that burned inside her.

Except Adrien beat her to it. "Monsieur, might there be a priest in the village? Or someone else authorized to perform marriages?"

Their guide turned to look at them over his shoulder, his gaze taking them in with a glimmer. He might have a smile buried under that wooly beard. "There is a priest here. He wintered with us and is planning to convert the Indians as soon as spring sets in a little better."

Mary's heart thrummed faster in her chest. *A priest.* Only God could have brought such a man to this far-flung outpost at this precise time.

"You want to see him first, or should I take you to a place you can settle your things?"

Adrien met her gaze, that face she loved so dearly. He appeared to be leaving the decision to her.

She inhaled a deep breath. "Maybe if we could care for the mule first, and borrow water and a rag."

The man chortled. "The best water's in the river over there. We can see to your animal."

Adrien was his usual considerate self as he extracted the things she requested from Domino's packs, then sent her toward the river. "I'm not sure how much privacy you'll have, but I'll keep a watch. Just call if you need anything."

In other words, this wasn't the time for a full dunking. The water was frigid enough she wouldn't have attempted it anyway, so she cleaned herself the best she could.

She'd like to change into her dress before the ceremony, if she could secure a moment alone in one of the buildings. With the men all doing a poor job of hiding their curiosity as she approached the structures, privacy might be hard to come by in this place.

Adrien met her at the corner of a shack. "They've offered this building for us to stay the night. It will at least suffice for the day. Later, we can decide if we want to sleep here or down the trail."

Sleep. She couldn't quite meet his gaze, not with the heat flooding her face. "Is it empty just now?"

He nodded, a corner of his mouth tipping. "I can stand outside to make sure it stays so."

A small bit of relief sank through her. "*Merci.*"

When she settled the clean muslin dress in place, its fabric felt foreign to her skin so accustomed to leathers. The change was good for this day. This most special of days.

Adrien spoke to a man as she stepped from the building, and both of them turned to her. Her groom opened his mouth as though about to speak, but he stalled, his gaze sliding the length of her. She'd seen that look of male appreciation before, but it had never ignited the kind of cozy warmth that now spread all the way through her. "Mary, may I introduce you to Father Bergeron? He's the missionary priest who's been staying here."

She turned to the other man, who was maybe a decade or so older than Adrien. But he had the same smile lines creasing the corners of his eyes. Kindly eyes.

She stepped forward and allowed him to press her hand.

"It is an honor, Mademoiselle. I am most pleased to meet you both." He straightened. "I've been asking much about the Indian tribes in this area, and am intrigued by those near the mountains from which you've come. Perhaps you can tell me more of them?"

She glanced at Adrien. "I can tell you what I've seen. Did Adrien make our request of you?"

Adrien's gaze held a merriment that told her he had, but it was the priest who answered.

"Indeed. I would be honored to perform the ceremony when you're ready."

She straightened, releasing a long breath as her eyes sought those she loved again. "I think we're ready now."

~

*A*drien stroked his thumb over Mary's hand as they stood at the river's edge, facing Father Bergeron. After months of dreaming, yearning for this moment, they had arrived.

Today. *Now.* This woman was becoming his bride. It was almost too much to fathom.

With her head bowed to receive the priest's blessing, he couldn't help but study her. Dark lashes brushed her cheeks, her full lips moved as though silently speaking. Praying?

His own soul quickened. *So much you've given me, Lord. My heart overflows.*

When they spoke the final "Amen" and the priest gave him leave to kiss her, Mary turned her lovely face up to him. For just a moment, he studied her. Drinking her in. The love in her beautiful blue gaze.

Then he lowered his mouth, taking an extra breath to savor the touch of her. With effort, he kept the kiss chaste. Simply a promise of more to come.

As he pulled away, her eyes were shining.

"Are you ready to journey home, Madame Lockman?" He had to work to force the words through the emotion clogging his throat.

She looked like an angel, smiling at him like that. "I am. Our home. Together."

Did you enjoy Adrien and Mary's story? I hope so!
Would you take a quick minute to leave a review?
It doesn't have to be long. Just a sentence or two telling what you liked about the story!

~

And would you like to receive a **free short story about a special moment in Gideon and Leah's happily-ever after?**
Get the free short story and sign-up for insider email updates by tapping here.

And here's a peek at the next book in the series, *This Courageous Journey*:

AUGUST, 1858
MONTANA TERRITORY

Noelle's Journal:

August 12th

Today, we left the train—forever, if my aching limbs decided the matter. The Lord's mercies are new every day, as the Psalmist wrote, but I think today's relief from that filthy, rattling car may be the greatest mercy the Father has offered in recent centuries.

We couldn't have chosen a more inspiring place in which to disembark. The grassland stretches as far as I can see, all the way to the edge of the sky. Flat at first, then ruffled in hills, like creases marring a smooth linen cloth. Elmer says we'll be traveling straight north, and he's purchased a wagon to carry us.

I think, perhaps, I'll be walking much of the way. Tomorrow is far too soon to be sentenced to days on end of another shaking conveyance. I imagine Louise will be eager to stretch her limbs as well, although she looked so pretty when she mounted the wagon bench and sat beside Elmer. The pair of them as much in love as they were a half-dozen summers ago on their wedding day. Bo stuck his tousled little head between them, his gap-toothed smile as bright as the freckles splashed across his cheeks. Were I to ever consider marriage, I should dream of a portrait just like they formed.

Yet, I'm not foolish enough to see only the loveliness. The lifetime of domesticity may suit many, but I'll not resign myself to being merely a shadow behind a man. I want more. Greater things. I want to stand out.

I think...the beating in my breast seems to know...this journey is the beginning of greater things. My skin tingles with anticipation. Soon, I will meet face-to-face with my destiny.

Noelle Grant closed the leather-bound journal and pressed the cover flat as she stared out across the world around her. Were those mountains in the distance? Almost all of Simeon's letters had mentioned mountains, so this flat land must mean they weren't even close yet.

"Noelle. Come, I want you to meet someone." Louise's voice pierced her focus, and Noelle turned to meet her friend. "Elmer finally found a guide to take us the rest of the way to your brother's home in Canada."

Noelle allowed her friend to tug her elbow, guiding her back toward the cluster of people and buildings that made up this muddy train stop. "Has he said how long the rest of our journey will take?"

"Not that I heard. But Elmer's thinking three or four weeks at the most."

A surge of anticipation swelled in her chest. Another month and she'd finally see her brother again. And meet his new family. Simeon had been away from home so long, yet she'd not stopped missing her protective elder brother. The oldest in their brood of nine siblings, but he'd always had a way of making her feel special. Like she was more than just one of the many.

"There they are." Elmer's gravelly voice broke through her thoughts as he turned to face them, allowing a view of the man to whom he spoke. "Mr. Abrams, meet the other member of our party. Miss Noelle Grant."

He stood tall, dressed in buckskins from head to toe, and a darker fur cap on his head. Substantial, with those broad shoulders and feet spread as though he braced to withstand attack. A beard fringed his face, and his eyes narrowed as he took her in, making it impossible to read his expression.

She dipped a slight curtsey. "A pleasure to meet you, Mr. Abrams."

His nod was barely perceptible. "Ma'am." Then he turned back to Elmer. "Can you leave at first light?" And just like that, she'd been dismissed. Not worth bothering over for more than a simple word.

She turned away from the men. Someday she'd make a name for herself that would stand out when she was introduced. Someday she would be more than just another face in the crowd.

Something pushed at her skirts, and she stepped back, looking down to see what she'd rubbed against.

Dark, soulful eyes stared up at her from the furry face of a dog. He pressed against her skirt again, and she reached down to stroke his head. "Hey, there." The dog's fluffy hair sported patches of black and brown and white, and as she rubbed behind his ear, his tongue lolled out in a contented pant.

A sharp whistle pierced the air, and the dog jerked to attention, whirling from her.

Noelle searched for the source, her gaze landing on their guide, who scowled at the animal and pointed to the ground by his foot. The dog circled and sat in that exact spot, then looked back at her, those dark eyes seeming to question. He tilted his head, adding to the inquisitive look. *Who are you?* he seemed to ask. *And why can't we be friends?*

She raised her gaze to the man. "He wasn't bothering me. I like animals."

He didn't answer, just eyed her. Scrutinizing, as though taking her measure.

Frustration built in her chest. Did this man have a single bone of civility in him?

A feminine throat cleared, reining in her thoughts. Pricking the surge of frustration so it eased out of her like spent air. Louise was right. They needed this man's help to get to Simeon. Whether he possessed proper conversational manners or not, didn't signify. As long as he didn't make improper advances.

A knot tried to form in her middle, but she pushed it down with the thought. She'd be on guard, and Elmer would too, certainly.

And now they'd obtained this last critical requirement, they could start out tomorrow. Soon, she'd be on her way to visit her long lost brother, and hopefully, uncover some terrific stories along the way. Stories that would propel her to journalistic renown.

Stories she could tell in a way that would prove she was someone special.

Daniel Abrams strode away from the crowd of people and buildings that tried to call itself a town. His spirit craved the peace away from all that bustle and talking.

Now that he had things lined up for his next foray north, he could relax. Maybe take a swim in the river to clean up. This might be his last chance in water that didn't steal his breath with its icy chill. Heading back into the Canadian territories would be a relief, though. Back to the land he'd traversed a thousand times during his growing-up days.

The land of his father.

Although that wasn't the case anymore, since the man's death. Yet it was hard to think of those mountains and rivers as anything other than his father's domain. Even while his soul longed for that land, he had to fight the urge to flee from it. This time, he would be good enough. Even though the one who mattered would no longer be there to see it.

At the water's edge, he stripped off his hat, tunic, and moccasins, leaving only his breeches. Griz bounced at his feet, knowing what was coming. "You wanna join me, boy?" He tousled the animal's head and received a sloppy lick on his arm. "Come on in."

The water wasn't deep enough to dive from the shore, so Daniel waded in to his waist. On the bank, Griz barked and pounced. "Come on." Daniel slapped his leg.

With a flying leap, the dog dove into the water, landing with a splash before his legs started paddling furiously. Daniel pushed aside the weight on his chest and chuckled at the sight the dog made, then sank down in the water to his chin. The chill invigorated his senses, making his blood surge.

After ducking under the surface, he came up with a splash to meet Griz, nose-to-nose. The dog barked, spraying slobbery water in his face. "Oh, ho." Daniel returned it with a light splash.

The dog blew into the water in a way that appeared suspiciously like a return volley. "You wanna play like that, do ya?"

He splashed a few drops back at the animal, but his mind slipped back to the woman whom Griz approached earlier. He'd always heard white women could be fragile and skittish, easily frightened by a wooly, bear-like dog such as Griz. His instincts had been to shield her from the dog, and the dog from her. Yet the look on her face had almost seemed hurt, like he'd insulted her.

That hadn't been his intent, but he'd obviously missed the mark. He so rarely spoke with women of any race, and almost never with white women. It appeared he'd have to be more careful.

Griz finally tired of their splashing game and headed back to shore. Daniel took the quiet moment to lay back in the water, floating half-covered by its surface. Just the solitude he needed to focus his mind on the job ahead.

He never particularly liked work as a guide. So much harder to be responsible for other people than when he was on his own, trapping and trading with the Indians. But the pay was decent, and since he was headed toward the Canadian mountains anyway, accepting this job was smart business.

If only Biggers didn't insist on taking that wagon. With the conveyance, they'd have to skirt some of the mountains, which would add time to the trip. It'd be so much easier and safer to use pack horses instead, even if they had to buy a few extra animals. But the man wouldn't hear of it. Said the women and boy would need a place to ride.

Which was another thing. Did they really know what they were getting into, heading into the mountain wilderness as they planned? These easterners probably wouldn't last a year where they were traveling. At least, not the women.

He straightened in the water and pressed his feet into the muddy river bottom, then scrubbed wet hands over his face.

Guiding them north was one thing. Keeping them alive to finish the journey was a whole different obstacle. He'd have his work cut out for him.

Get THIS COURAGEOUS JOURNEY at your favorite retailer.

ABOUT THE AUTHOR

Misty M. Beller is a *USA Today* bestselling author of romantic mountain stories, set on the 1800s frontier and woven with the truth of God's love.

Raised on a farm and surrounded by family, Misty developed her love for horses, history, and adventure. These days, her husband and children provide fresh adventure every day, keeping her both grounded and crazy.

Misty's passion is to create inspiring Christian fiction infused with the grandeur of the mountains, writing historical romance that displays God's abundant love through the twists and turns in the lives of her characters.

Sharing her stories with readers is a dream come true for Misty. She writes from her country home in South Carolina and escapes to the mountains any chance she gets.

Connect with Misty at <u>www.MistyMBeller.com</u>

ALSO BY MISTY M. BELLER

Call of the Rockies
Freedom in the Mountain Wind
Hope in the Mountain River
Light in the Mountain Sky
Courage in the Mountain Wilderness
Faith in the Mountain Valley
Honor in the Mountain Refuge
Peace in the Mountain Haven
Grace on the Mountain Trail
Calm in the Mountain Storm

Brides of Laurent
A Warrior's Heart
A Healer's Promise
A Daughter's Courage

Hearts of Montana
Hope's Highest Mountain
Love's Mountain Quest
Faith's Mountain Home

Texas Rancher Trilogy
The Rancher Takes a Cook
The Ranger Takes a Bride
The Rancher Takes a Cowgirl

Wyoming Mountain Tales

A Pony Express Romance

A Rocky Mountain Romance

A Sweetwater River Romance

A Mountain Christmas Romance

The Mountain Series

The Lady and the Mountain Man

The Lady and the Mountain Doctor

The Lady and the Mountain Fire

The Lady and the Mountain Promise

The Lady and the Mountain Call

This Treacherous Journey

This Wilderness Journey

This Freedom Journey (novella)

This Courageous Journey

This Homeward Journey

This Daring Journey

This Healing Journey

Printed in Great Britain
by Amazon

35185248R00065